OWJC
11/13

Using Scommun   e
myster

Hmmm. I didn't know if he could understand me, but I sure wasn't understanding him. We both seemed to be speaking in a foreign tongue, but not necessarily the same one. Or...wait. Perhaps I had forgotten some of the vocabulary. I mean, it wasn't every day that I carried on a conversation in Speaklish.

I would have to keep trying. "Eecher-cray: utt-whey iz-yeah oour-yeah aim-nay? Awk-tay."

I waited for his reply, and this time, it came loud and clear. He said, "Oom-pah oom-pah Ort-snay."

The "oom-pah oom-pah" meant nothing to me, but *Ort-snay*? The word had a familiar ring, but for a moment or two, I couldn't get the cart before the hammer. I did a quick search of my memory banks and came up with a match.

Ort-snay was the Speaklish word for... SNORT!

The Ghost of Rabbits Past

John R. Erickson

Illustrations by Gerald L. Holmes

Maverick Books, Inc.

MAVERICK BOOKS, INC.
Published by Maverick Books, Inc.
P.O. Box 549, Perryton, TX 79070
Phone: 806.435.7611
www.hankthecowdog.com

First published in the United States of America by Maverick Books, Inc. 2013.

1 3 5 7 9 10 8 6 4 2

Copyright © John R. Erickson, 2013

All rights reserved

LIBRARY OF CONGRESS CONTROL NUMBER: 2013947560

978-1-59188-162-9 (paperback); 978-1-59188-262-6 (hardcover)

Hank the Cowdog® is a registered trademark of John R. Erickson.

Printed in the United States of America

Except in the United States of America, this book is sold subject
to the condition that it shall not, by way of trade or otherwise, be lent,
re-sold, hired out, or otherwise circulated without the publisher's
prior consent in any form of binding or cover other than that in which
it is published and without a similar condition including this
condition being imposed on the subsequent purchaser.

*I dedicate this book to the memory of
C.S. Lewis, in appreciation for the education
I have gotten from his books.
I think he would have liked Hank.*

CONTENTS

CHAPTER ONE

We're Attacked By Hoodian Voles!

It's me again, Hank the Cowdog. We're going to take this story one step at a time and we're going to start at the beginning. Are you ready for that? You'd better be, because the train's fixing to leave the station, and I'll tell you right now, it's going to be scary.

Okay, here we go. The moment I heard the eerie scream, I knew we had a problem. I had been out most of the night, doing a routine patrol of ranch headquarters, and had returned to the office to work my way through a stack of reports. On this outfit, the work of the Security Division never ends. If we're not walking the beat, we're tied up with paperwork.

Maybe I had dozed off at my desk. Yes, of

course I had dozed off. That's what dogs do when they finish an eighteen-hour shift. We try to exceed the limits imposed by flesh and blood, but sometimes sleep creeps up from behind and grabs us.

I'd fallen into a light doze, is the point, but came roaring out of it when I heard the terrible screams. I leaped to my feet and hit Sirens and Lights. "Speckled starfish in the rectangular salad! Man the lifeboats and don't forget the ketchup!"

I made a dash for the lifeboats but ran into one of the sailors in the dark. It knocked both of us to the deck. I sat up and so did the other party. I narrowed my eyes and studied his face. "Are you going to lower the lifeboats or just sit there?"

"I don't think we have any lifeboats."

"They're already gone? Why wasn't I informed? How can I command this ship if it's sinking all the time?" I blinked my eyes and glanced around. "Are we sinking?"

"I don't think so. You need water to sink."

"You saw water in the sink? Where is the sink?"

"I don't know, in the bathroom, I guess."

"That fits, but where's the bathroom?"

"Out in the weeds."

"We have weeds in the bathroom?"

"We don't have a bathroom."

"Already I've found a fly in your oatmeal. If we don't have a bathroom, we can't possibly have a sink...and by the way, who are you?"

He grinned. "Drover. Hi."

I looked closer and recognized his face. "Hi. We need to get those lifeboats in the water, fast."

"We don't have any."

"No lifeboats? What kind of ship is this?"

"It's our bedroom. You're still asleep."

I leaned toward him and whispered, "I'll try to forget you said that."

"Thanks."

"Drover, where are we?"

"Under the gas tanks."

I paced a few steps away and tried to clear the fog out of my head. "Who started this rumor about the sinking ship? I must know."

"It wasn't me."

"Then who or whom does that leave as a suspect?"

"I think you were dreaming."

"I was NOT dreaming."

"Yeah, but there's nobody left to blame."

I shot him a cunning smile. "That's where you're wrong, son. We've always got the cat."

"You mean...Pete?"

"Exactly. Don't forget: he specializes in lies, gossip, and dirty tricks."

"Yeah, but..."

"At this point, we don't know how he did it, but all the evidence points at him like a flaming arrow."

"What's the evidence?"

"The evidence is that we have no evidence, which is irreguffable proof that a cat was behind this whole charade."

He yawned. "I'll be derned."

"Please don't yawn while I'm reviewing a case."

"Sorry."

"It's very discouraging when I look out at the audience and see dogs who are yawning."

"Sorry, but it's the middle of the night."

"That is not my fault, Drover. I don't pick the times when the cat chooses to sabotage our systems."

"Can I go back to bed?"

"No, not until we make some progress on this case." I began pacing, as I often do when my mind is racing after the Rabbit of Truth. "Okay, make a note and enter it into the Daily Log. The Sinking Ship Episode was a fraud from start to finish, a distraction created by the cat to disrupt our systems. At our first opportunity, we will thrash the little snot and park him in a tree. Make three copies and post one on the bulletin board."

He glanced around. "Where's the bulletin board?"

"Drover, I deal in large concepts. You figure out the bulletin boards. Now, unless you have further questions, I'd like to get some sleep."

"Can I yawn now?"

"Yes. Yawn all you want. Fall into your yawns, I don't care, just don't make any noise."

I rumbled over to my gunny sack, fluffed it up, and collapsed. Exhaustion leaped upon me like a lurking tiger. I was drifting off when I heard an odd sound. It was Drover, yawning. "Boy, that was a good one. I love to yawn. I'd rather yawn than chew a bone. There's another good one!"

I sat up and melted him with a glare. "Drover, if you continue making noise, we will have to impose a ban on yawning. Is that what you want?"

That got his attention. "Gosh, I don't know what I'd do if I couldn't yawn."

"I'm sure it would become a personal crisis, so yawn quietly. And don't mutter about how much

you love to yawn."

"Okay, sorry. I'll try."

"Good night."

At last he shut his beak and I began drifting out on the snorking honk of barbecued snicklefritz fiddle blossoms and spiral tomatoes...I must have dozed off, but not for long. All at once, another horrible scream penetrated the perpitude of my turpentine.

I shot straight up and staggered to my feet. "Drover, did you hear something?"

"Affirmative."

"A scream?"

His eyes were wide with fear. "Yeah, and it wasn't me."

"Then who could it..." And then we heard it again: an unearthly scream that made my hair stand on end. It wasn't Drover's yawning, and it wasn't the cat. "Good grief, what is that?"

Drover moved his lips but couldn't utter a sound, until at last he gasped, "I think it's the Hoodian Voles!"

Those words sent a scorching jolt of electricity down my spine. "Hoodian Voles! Do we have those things on this ranch?"

"Yeah, I saw five of 'em, right over there. They're everywhere!"

"You saw five Hoodian Voles?"

"Twenty-five."

"Good grief. What are they? Give me a description. Facts, we need facts and details."

His teeth were clacking together. "They looked just like twenty-five monsters, only ten times worse."

A wave of fear washed over me. "Okay, let's settle down. We've got to be professional about this."

"Yeah, let's head for the bunkers."

"I agree. To the bunkers!"

And so it began. We had ourselves an invasion of...whatever Drover had said, some kind of creatures, and you're probably worried sick. You should be. This had turned into a very dangerous night on our ranch.

CHAPTER TWO

Something Big and Hairy

The first reports were sketchy, but we had reason to think that a force of Hoodian Voles had overrun ranch headquarters and captured the barn and chicken house. I had never gone up against a Hoodian Vole, but our intelligence units had warned us that they were more dangerous than skeletons, ghosts, or monsters.

We responded in a professional manner and dived into our bunkers, the heavily fortified areas beneath our gunny sack beds. Once there, we closed the hatches and waited for something to happen. In the deadly silence, we heard a burst of high-pitched screeching and cackling.

Pretty scary, huh? You bet. Hey, I'm no chicken liver and over the course of my career, I'd heard some creepy sounds, but this! It was goose-bump creepy. For several moments, we listened as the sounds changed from hideous cackles into howls.

Drover was the first to speak. "You know what? That sounds like coyotes."

"Don't be absurd. Coyotes never come up this close to the house. And besides, your report stated that you saw twenty-five...whatever you called them."

"Hoodian Voles?"

"Exactly. Follow the trail of logic. If you witnessed an invasion of Hoodian Voles, that's what we're hearing."

"Yeah, but sometimes my eyes play tricks."

I glared at him in the darkness of the bunker. Actually, it was so dark in there, I couldn't see him, but I glared anyway. "Drover, is it possible that you turned in a garbled report?"

"I'd hate to put it that way."

"How would you put it?"

"Well, it was dark...and I was scared and half-asleep...and I thought I saw something, but maybe there weren't twenty-five of them."

"All right, maybe you miscounted. How many did you see?"

"Maybe five or three or only one. Or maybe I

didn't see anything."

I was stunned. "Drover, the first thing we need to clear up is...what exactly is a Hoodian Vole?"

"I don't know. It just popped into my head."

"It just popped...DID YOU SEE ANYTHING OR NOT?"

I heard him sniffling in the darkness. "No."

"Then why did you...I can't believe this!"

"I wanted to do something important. I thought you'd be proud of me."

"Proud! Do you realize the full impact of your bungling?"

"Yeah, I'm a failure."

"No, it's worse than that. You've made the entire Security Division look like...I don't know what. An outside observer would probably think this ranch is being run by monkeys."

"I'm sorry. I want to go home!"

"You are home."

"Then I want to go homer!"

"Stop blubbering. Once you've spilled the milk, it's too late to feed the horses."

"What does that mean?"

"I don't know. I'm babbling, you're babbling, the Security Division is in shambles..." I had to give myself a minute to absorb all of this. "All right, Drover, listen carefully. We must form a plan and stick with it. Number one, no more behaving like monkeys."

"I wish I had a banana."

"What?"

"I said, I'll try."

"Good. Number two, we will leave the bunkers. Number three, once we're outside, I don't know what we'll do, but we'll do something. Are you ready?"

"I guess."

"All right, stand by to put our plan into action. On my mark, we will leave the bunkers. Three, two, one, exit bunkers!"

We climbed out of the bunkers and found ourselves...well, in our office under the gas tanks. I lifted Earatory Scanners and did a sweep for sounds. I heard two crickets and an owl, but nothing that suggested skeletons, coyotes, or those other things. Hooligan Moles.

"Drover, the radar is clear, not a sound out there. Is it possible...do you suppose we dreamed all of this?"

"I sure thought I heard something scary."

"Right, and you thought you saw twenty-five Hooligan Moles, then admitted that you saw nothing. In the middle of the night, we can't trust your reports."

"Gosh, what'll we do?"

"We need some boots-on-the-ground reconnaissance."

"Boy, that's a big word."

"Any volunteers for a scout patrol?"

"I don't think I could even spell it."

"Spell what?"

"That word you just said."

"It's easy. S-C-O-U-T."

"No, the other word."

"P-A-T-R-O-L."

"No, the other one, the big one."

I stuck my nose in his face. "Life is not a spelling bee and we have serious work to do. We're looking for volunteers to make a scout patrol." Silence. Drover's eyes avoided my steely gaze. "The payoff could be huge: stripes, medals, stars, bars, certificates, promotions, double dog food...you name it. We're talking about hitting the jackpot."

"I think I'll pass."

"Drover, in this time of crisis, the ranch needs us."

"You'll go too?"

"Huh? Well, I...someone needs to stay here to coordinate the mission."

"Yeah, that's for me."

"That's not for you!" I paced a few steps away and tried to control the swirl of my thoughts. "All right, you little slacker, I'll go too, but you have to promise me one thing."

"Okay, I promise."

"I haven't said it yet."

"Oh, sorry."

I marched back and glared down into his face. "Promise you won't take off running and hide in the machine shed."

His eyes grew round with surprise. "How'd you know that's what I was going to do?"

"Because I know you. Because you do it all the time."

He grinned. "Gosh, I thought I was being sneaky."

"You're not smart enough to be sneaky, and besides, you're doing business with the Head of Ranch Sneakurity. I've seen it all, son. Now, promise on your Solemn Cowdog Oath that you won't run off and hide in the machine shed."

He stood up straight and raised his right front paw. "I promise NOT to NOT run off and hide in the machine shed."

"Good. It's done. Let's move out."

We grabbed weapons and ammo belts, left the

barracks, and marched off to the northeast, the direction from which the horrible sounds had come...if we'd actually heard any horrible sounds. Let's be honest. Things get confusing when we're jerked back and forth, from asleep to alert. Add Drover to the mix and you get something close to sheer chaos.

Remember what he'd said about loading the kitchen sink into a lifeboat? It was all crazy nonsense, but that's the kind of mess I have to deal with every day. Sometimes I can laugh about this stuff, but...well, remember the Wise Old Saying?

"Once in a while, it really matters that everyone on the team has the same grasp of reality."

That's a very wise Wise Old Saying, and you probably ought to write it down.

So there we were, marching through darkness, on a mission to gather reconnaissance about whatever had interrupted our sleep. By the time we arrived at the yard gate, we had seen nothing suspicious, and I had pretty muchly decided that we had dreamed the entire episode.

That's when I ran into something in the dark, something that shouldn't have been there. I reached for the radio. "Cottage Cheese, this is Chainsaw. We've encountered something in the dark. Description: large and hairy. What is your location? Over."

The radio crackled, then I heard a faint reply. "I'm outa here!"

"Cottage Cheese? Repeat that, over." The radio went silent. "Drover? I need your coordinates at once. Drover?"

Dead silence. My mind was tumbling. Was it possible that the little sneak had...wait a second! Remember Drover's Solemn Pledge? I hit the replay button and listened to it again.

"I promise NOT to NOT run off and hide in the machine shed."

Do you see the meaning of this? Let's go to the blackboard and write down the equation.

Not + Not = 0.

Do you get it now? Two *nots* cancel each other out. Remove the knots from a knot hole and you get empty space. Remove the *nots* from Drover's so-called pledge and you get, "I promise **to run off** and hide in the machine shed."

Are you shocked? I was. Maybe I should have expected some kind of treachery, but old, trusting Hank had gotten himself blind-sided. The magnitude of Drover's corruption left me dizzy and speechless, and don't tell me that I should have been listening more carefullier. Care-full-lee-er. More careful. Don't tell me that I should have...phooey.

Hey, I knew what he was *supposed* to say, and he knew what he was supposed to say, only he used a cheap trick and didn't say it. Before my very eyes and ears, he promised on his Cowdog Oath *to run off to the machine shed and hide.* And then he did it!

How did that make me look?

Oh brother. Sometimes I'm overwhelmed by the wickedness of this world—lies, cheating, dirty tricks, friend against friend, comrade against comrade. It almost broke my heart.

But I had bigger problems than a broken heart. If you recall, I had walked into something big and hairy in the darkness...and I wasn't anxious to find out what it might be.

CHAPTER THREE

Yipes!

A re you feeling nervous about this? Good. I was scared out of my wits.

All the evidence in this case suggested that I had either bumped into a cannibal, a Charlie Monster, or a Hooligan Mole. If you were in that situation, which would you choose?

Those were the choices I faced, only I really didn't have a choice, because whatever I'd bumped into was whatever it was, regardless of my opinions. That doesn't make sense, so let's move along.

The point is that I was out there alone in the darkness and had encountered some living *thing* that wasn't supposed to be there, and fellers, I had a real bad feeling about it. I tried to calm myself and plot a response. Should I bark the alarm, run, fight, or try to establish communication with the creature? Or creatures. For all I knew, there might be hundreds of them lurking in the darkness.

I ran these options through Data Control and got a green light for Communication. That made sense. Communicating with alien beings is much better than any of the other things you can do with them.

Trying to hide the quiver in my voice, I sent out a message.

"Hello there. This is the voice of the ranch's Security Division. You seem to be walking through a secured area without permission. If you're here by mistake, this doesn't have to be a big deal. Just turn around and leave the compound, and don't come back.

"If you came with hostile intentions, you should understand that we have snipers on the walls and three divisions of heavy infantry standing by. Any hostile action on your part will be met with deadly force."

I waited for a reply. Nothing, not a word, but I could hear raspy breathing, so I knew he was there. Suddenly it occurred to me that the creature might not speak Ranch English, so I tried another approach.

Have I mentioned that I'm effluent in many languages? I am. It's one of those skills that a top-of-the-line cowdog must be prepared to use in the course of a normal day. See, we never know the cultural background or language system of the Bad Guys we encounter on the ranch, so we must be prepared to conduct our business in any one of five or six languages.

I addressed him in Universal Speaklish. "Ooo-hay are-yea oo-yea, eecher-cray? Eek-spay."

This time I got a reply. "Oom-pah oom-pah."

"Utt-whey? Eeek-spay owder-lay."

"Oom-pah oom-pah, tic-tac-toe."

Hmmm. I didn't know if he could understand me, but I sure wasn't understanding him. We both seemed to be speaking in a foreign tongue, but not necessarily the same one. Or...wait. Perhaps I had forgotten some of the vocabulary. I mean, it wasn't every day that I carried on a conversation in Speaklish.

I would have to keep trying. "Eecher-cray: utt-whey iz-yeah oour-yeah aim-nay? Awk-tay."

I waited for his reply, and this time, it came loud and clear. He said, "Oom-pah oom-pah Ort-snay."

The "oom-pah oom-pah" meant nothing to me,

but *Ort-snay*? The word had a familiar ring, but for a moment or two, I couldn't get the cart before the hammer. I did a quick search of my memory banks and came up with a match.

Ort-snay was the Speaklish word for... SNORT!

At that same moment, I began to notice a heavy musky odor in the aerosphere. Gulp. In the darkness of night, I had just made contact with a notorious cannibal named Snort, who had a notorious cannibal brother named Rip. And they were both notorious cannibals.

Encantering countables in the dark of night might be better than encumbering vegetables... sorry, let me back up and start that sentence again. Encountering cannibals in the dark of night might be better than encountering vampires, but it's not exactly something to celebrate.

See, I had done business with Rip and Snort, and knew them fairly well—as well as a dog can ever know the murky depths of a cannibal's mind. If you caught them at the right moment, on the right day, they could be a barrel of laughs. You talk about a couple of goof-offs! They were worthless beyond all description and did things that normal dogs only dream about.

They were experts at scratching fleas. They

composed trashy coyote songs and could howl all night long. Their belching skills were the stuff of legends. They knew everything there was to know about rolling on a dead skunk and impressing the ladies with their deep manly aroma. They got into fights, beat up badgers, and banged their heads against trees just for sport. And nobody could beat them when it came to poaching chickens. Slurp. Excuse me.

Please ignore that "slurp." It meant almost nothing.

The point is that when Rip and Snort were in a friendly mood, they became role models and the envy of every ranch dog in Texas—because they were bums, totally worthless, no ambition, no jobs, no duties or responsibilities, just goofing off forever.

But there was the Other Side, where good old boys passed through a veil of darkness and became bad old boys, and their true coyote nature overpowered everything else. With Rip and Snort, it was a short step from one side to the other. One minute would find them full of fun and nonsense, and the next...yipes. Their eyes began to sparkle with unholy yellow light, and a ranch dog began to realize...*these guys might eat a dog*!

So there you are, a glance at our files on Rip and Snort. And there I was, all alone in the darkness with Snort, and probably not far from Rip, since they always ran together.

It was too late to escape. There was no place to hide. I didn't know which mood they were in. I would have to try to get out of this with charm and diplomacy.

I tried to put a little jingle into my voice. "Hey Snort, is that you?"

"Ha! Me, you betcha, and brother too. Rip and Snort come to town and take over whole place."

"Well, it isn't actually a town, Snort. It's only the headquarters compound of our ranch, but to you guys, it must seem like a huge and busy place."

"Plenty huge and dizzy."

"No, I said *busy*. Biz, biz, biz. Bizz-zee. Dizzy is something else."

"Hunk quit talk like beetle-bum."

"A what? Oh, you mean a bumblebee?"

"Rip and Snort not friend to beetle-bum, get stung on nose."

"Right. Those beetle-bums are bad news."

"Hunk get bad news if keeping talk like beetle-bum."

"Sorry. I didn't realize you were so sensitive.

Let's talk about something else. What brings you to ranch headquarters? I mean, you guys don't come here very often."

"Uh. 'Cause guys not like house and boom-boom."

"Right. Coyotes are scared of people and guns."

"Coyotes not scared of nothing."

"That's what I meant. You're not scared of anything, but you'd rather not get peppered with buckshot."

"Rip and Snort not give a hoot for pepper."

"I agree. It'll burn your mouth and make you sneeze, and raise your temperature twenty degrees. Ha ha. A little humor there, a rhyme for the evening, so to speak. Ha ha."

There was a long, deadly silence. "Hunk try to be funny?"

"Well, yes. I just thought...hey Snort, let's be honest. Talking with you can be pretty depressing."

"Ha! Coyote brothers not give a hoot for pretty dressing. Coyote brothers ugly and meaner than whole world."

"That was my point. You guys are ugly and mean, and sometimes I find that depressing."

"Hunk talk too much. Rip and Snort come on important mitchen."

Mitchen? Hmmm. I wasn't familiar with that word, but it must have been important, because... well, because he'd said so, right? "Important mitchen." Wait, I had it! In the coyote dialect, *mitchen* translated into *mission*.

"Oh, I get it now. You're here on an important mission?"

"Mitchen. Hunk not know how to talk."

"Sorry, my fault. You're here on an important *mitchen*. Would it be proper for me to ask the nature of your mitchen?"

"Brothers come to catnip kid."

"You're calling yourself the Catnip Kid? Gee, that's nice, Snort, I like it. Every outlaw ought to have a nickname."

Snort grumbled, "What means 'nick-nock'?"

At that moment, the moon appeared from behind a layer of clouds and...yipes, I got my first glimpse of the cannibals. They towered over me and were beaming glares that seemed irritated and unfriendly, even hostile.

"I didn't say nick-nock. I said nickname, and a nickname is...well, it's a name we give ourselves in a spirit of fun or affection."

"Snort not have fun with infection, too many germs."

You know, under different circumstances, I

would have been laughing. I mean, this was the craziest conversation I'd had since the last time I'd tried to communicate with these boneheads. But laughing in front of cannibals wasn't something I wanted to try.

Let's face it, being incredibly dumb isn't always funny to those who are.

Hencely, laughing was out of the question, but somehow I had to keep the conversation moving. Don't forget, when cannibals stop talking, they start thinking about food.

But what could I say?

CHAPTER FOUR

The Catnip Kid

Tough assignment, right? You bet. This conversation had not only gone off the rails, there weren't any rails left. Snort had a genius for misunderstanding every word and turning every conversation on its head. No ordinary dog could have kept going, but I did. Hey, I had no choice.

"Okay, Snort, I agree about the germs. We'll have no germs and no infections. Everything we say will be sanitary."

"Brothers not go to cemetery, got too many skeletons."

"Great point. Cemeteries are out, skeletons are out, and no more germs. But tell me this. Why did you decide to call yourself the Catnip

Kid?"

He stared at me with empty eyes. "Snort not call nobody Catnip Kid. Dummy dog not understand nothing for phooey. Rip and Snort come chopping for cat."

"You're chopping cats? I'm sorry, Snort, but that just doesn't make any..."

BAM! He clubbed me over the head with his paw. "Hunk better listen pretty quick or Snort break face. Brothers come to ranch to catnip kid."

For a moment, I was baffled. What in the world was he trying to...wait! Of course, don't you get it? They had come to ranch headquarters to...

I'm sure you didn't figure it out for yourself, because...well, you're not accustomed to dealing with cannibals and trying to translate their grunted gibberish into simple language that makes sense.

Okay, let's slow down and sort this out. Snort had muttered something about "catnip kid." You thought he had taken a new nickname and was now calling himself The Catnip Kid, as in "The Catnip Kid rides again!"

Nope, you had it figured all wrong. I picked it up right away and worked out the translation. Are you ready to hear it? Rip and Snort had come to ranch headquarters on a *mitchen* (remember, that's Coyote for "mission") to *kidnap the cat*.

Do you get it now? Cats love catnip, but coyotes love to kidnap, so when a coyote grumbles the phrase "catnip the kid," he's really saying that he wants to kidnap the cat.

It's kind of a backwards code, don't you see, and once you've broken their codes, the rest is easy.

Wow, what a shocking revelation. They wanted to steal the little slacker who hung out on my ranch—Pete the Barncat—and I must confess that my first thought was...

I'd better not say it. It might sound cruel and harsh and...look, this is my story and I don't have to reveal my true thoughts about Pete or anything else. Think of the little children. What would say if they knew that my first reaction to Snort's kidnapping plot was, "WHAT A DEAL!"

The kids would be shocked and disappointed. They would think that I'm a heartless lout. They would probably take the side of the kitty, even though they don't know him as well as I know him—that he's a scheming, back-stabbing little sneak.

No, I'm not going to reveal...wait. You know what? I already let it slip out. Did you notice?

Oh brother. Well, it's out in the open and there's no use in pretending. I've shot myself in the foot with my own big mouth, so we might as well hang out all the dirty laundry on the Clothes Line of Life.

Okay, when Snort revealed his plot to catnip the kid...kidnap the cat, that is, I reacted with an explosion of...this is going to sound bad, so hang on...I reacted with an explosion of pure laughter and joy.

WHAT A DEAL! In one big swoop, I could get a couple of dangerous cannibals away from headquarters and, at the same time, dispose of a nuisance that had dealt me misery for years.

I mean, this fit in perfectly with my Position on Cats. We've discussed my POC, right? I don't like 'em, never have and never will. My idea of a perfect day is a day without cats. My idea of a perfect ranch is a ranch without cats. My idea of a perfect business transaction is one that allows me to unload the local cat on a couple of cannibal thugs.

Hee, hee, hee. Fellers, this was going to be fun.

It took me a moment to regain my composure. "Snort, that is one of the greatest ideas I've ever heard, and I'll back you every step of the way. I'll give you the keys to the ranch. We'll turn off all security systems and you can make yourself right at home." I gave him a wink and a grin. "Hey, bud, I'll even tell you where to find the little pest."

"What wrongs with Hunk eyeball?"

"What? Nothing's wrong with my eyeball. I was winking at you."

"How come Hunk winkie eyeball at Snort?"

I took a deep breath and searched for patience. "Snort, I winked my eye as a little gesture of friendship, two guys sharing a joke."

"Snort not want to choke."

"Fine. We'll forget the whole thing. It's not important."

He glared at me. "Winkie eyeball make Snort berry suppishus of Hunk."

"Well, we don't want you to get suspicious."

"Suppishus. Hunk not know how to talk."

"Sorry. We don't want you to get suppishus."

"Hunk all the time talk like dummy."

"Okay, fine, whatever. Can we change the subject? You came here to kidnap the cat, so let's get on with it."

The brothers went into a whispering conference, then Snort said, "Brother still suppishus of winkie eyeball."

This was starting to get on my nerves. "What

is wrong with you guys? You get hung up on some little detail and you can't get away from it."

"Hunk close one eye, not winkie no more."

"I will *not* close one eye! That would be totally ridiculous." Snort raised his paw like a club. "Okay, no problem, I'll close one eye." I squeezed my left eye shut.

"Not winkie no more with other eyeball too."

"Fine. I will not winkie no more with other eyeball too. Now, where were we? You guys have got me so rattled, I don't know which way is up."

Snort pointed his paw toward the sky. "That way up." He pointed toward the ground. "That way down." He swung his paw in a circle. "That way all around."

"Thank you, Snort. I don't know how I've gotten along all these years without your help. Okay, you're shopping for a cat, right?"

The brothers shook their heads in unison. "Chopping for cat."

"Sorry. You're *chopping* for a cat, and I can help. He stays in the yard, right over there in the iris patch. Be my guest. Help yourselves." They stared at me with empty yellow eyes. "Now what's the problem?"

"Hunk fetch cat."

"Hey, this is your deal. I don't want to fetch

the cat."

Snort's hammer fist came down on top of my head. BAM! "Hunk fetch cat pretty quick or get snot beat out of!"

I picked myself off the ground and gave them a ragged smile. "Here's an idea. Why don't I fetch the cat?"

They howled with laughter. "Hunk fetch cat, and be quicker and quickest, oh boy!"

Well, this deal had gotten out of hand, but they'd left me with no choice. I would have to serve as their delivery dog. I hopped over the fence and started toward the iris patch. With every step, I felt...

You know, it's one thing to *talk* about bumping off the cat...wait, that sounds pretty bad. Let's try a different approach. It's one thing to talk about, uh, letting a couple of cannibals *borrow* your cat, and it's another to actually be involved in it. Pete had been a constant source of irritation to me for years, but...this?

By the time I reached the iris patch, I was not feeling good about it, but the brothers were watching my every move. What else could I do? I tried to remember every sneaky trick the cat had pulled on me, hoping it would help me through this time of trial.

I rumbled up to the iris patch, expecting the kitty to greet me with his usual insolent smirk and his annoying, "Well, well! It's Hankie the Wonderdog." That's not what he said. He said nothing, and it appeared that he was...

"What are you doing?"

He turned to me with a sad smile. "Oh, I was just tidying up my little nest. I..." A quiver came into his voice. "I guess I won't be coming back."

"What is that supposed to mean?"

"I heard everything. You have no choice." He glanced around and sighed. "I'll go without a struggle."

I was stunned. "What! That's crazy."

"I thought that's the way you would want it."

"You let me decide what I want, and stop butting into my..." My mind was reeling. I staggered a few steps away and gasped for air. "Pete, you have no idea what you're doing to me."

"I thought I was making it easy."

"Yeah? Well, you thought wrong. This ought to be the finest moment of my life, but somehow you've..." I stormed back over to him. "Listen, you little pestilence, I'm supposed to deliver you to the coyote brothers. They want to eat you. I want them to eat you. You drive me insane."

He shrugged. "Well, let's get on with it."

"We will NOT get on with it! I don't know how you've managed to do it, but you are about to ruin my life!"

"Poor doggie."

"Shut your trap. Those coyotes are on the other side of the fence. They're watching us. They're licking their chops and tapping their toes. They're getting hungry and restless. In ninety seconds, they will jump the fence and be on top of us."

"Well, just turn me in and let's get it over with. I've had a good life."

"Will you dry up? It would have been SO EASY, SO SIMPLE, if you had just been your usual unbearable self, but now...look what you've done! I can't go through with this!"

Snort's voice cut through the gloom of night like a chainsaw. "Hunk hurry up and fetch cat, or brothers get madder and maddest, and beat up whole world!"

Can you believe this? I couldn't believe it. I'd been offered the opportunity of a lifetime and I'd muffed it. I'd choked. I'd become a disgrace to the entire Security Division and to dogs all over Texas.

I stormed over to the rotten little creep who had caused this. "We've got about sixty seconds

before lightning strikes. What are we going to do?"

"Well, Hankie, I could climb a tree, but that wouldn't help you."

"That's correct. They would eat me, and you'd have to watch. Tell the truth, Pete, would you enjoy it?"

He grinned. "I'll get back to you on that. Maybe you should bark the alarm and wake up the house."

"Won't work, Pete. Loper's reaction time at this hour of the night runs about ten minutes."

"Darn."

"We've got thirty seconds. Shall we try to make a run for it?"

He shook his head. "I'm afraid there's no running from coyotes."

"Well...I guess we stand and fight. I figure we can hold out for about twelve seconds and then we're hamburger."

Our situation looked hopeless.

CHAPTER FIVE

Drover Is Catnipped

The cat held me in his gaze and gave me a peculiar smile. "This is odd, isn't it, Hankie, you and I fighting on the same side."

"It's worse than odd. It's unnatural. It's weird. My mother would be so disappointed if she could see me now."

"I know. All my cat kinfolks would be crushed."

"It's a lousy way to ring down the curtain of our lives."

"It really is."

"And it's all your fault, you little creep!" I stuck my nose in his face and gave him my Train Horns Bark. BWONK!

You know what he did? He humped his back, hissed, and...BAM...slapped me across the nose

40

with a handful of claws, stung like crazy and brought water to my eyes.

"That was for old times, Hankie."

"Thanks, Pete. You're a rotten little crook of a cat, but we did have some great moments. Are you ready for the grand finale?"

"Let the dance begin."

We turned toward the west and I sent out a press release to the Coyote Brotherhood, an announcement that would smell our foots. Our fates, that is, an announcement that would seal our fates.

"Hey Snort! The deal's off. I'm not your delivery boy, and you can't eat my cat. Furthermore, your momma's an ugly toad. Remember the Alamo!"

Boy, that woke 'em up. You never heard such an outburst of angry snarls and growls. Rip stood up on his hind legs and began pounding his chest, while Snort banged his head against the gate post. In the midst of all that, they were both screeching about the awful things they were going to do to us. Gulp. It gave me the shivers.

But then...you won't believe this part, I guarantee that you won't believe it...just then, guess who came out of the machine shed. Mister Half-Stepper. Mister Run and Hide. He yelled,

"Hank, be careful! I thought I heard some coyotes!"

A deathly silence fell over the ranch. The cannibals froze and turned like battleship guns toward the runt. When he saw their horrid yellow eyes and gleaming fangs, he...this was *so Drover*... he let out a squeak and FAINTED! I'm not kidding, he went over like a bicycle.

In an instant, and we're talking about the blink of an eye (or, to put into the Coyote Dialect, "in winkie of eyeball")...in the blink of a so-forth, the coyotes were all over him. Rip scooped up the little mutt in his jaws and Snort turned to us.

In a cackling voice, he yelled, "Ha! Rip and Snort not give a hoot for catnip kid! Make yum-yum out of little white dog, oh boy!"

And with that, they vanished into the night—carrying the poor, misguided, feather-brained Drover off to a fate we could only imagine.

I was too stunned to speak or move. It had happened so fast! One second, Pete and I were ready to fight the second battle of the Alamo, and the next second, Drover had been shanghaied by cannibals and carried off to the wilderness.

Pete was the first to speak. "Well! What shall we do now?"

I had to sit down. I mean, my legs were

shaking like...I don't know what, like shaking legs, I suppose. "I have no idea. I didn't expect to live this long."

"Should we try to follow them?"

"Into the wilderness? At night? That would be suicide. No, we'd better wait for..." I narrowed my eyes at the cat. "What do you mean, 'we'? I don't work with cats. It's immoral, indecent, unheard of, and against regulations."

"I know, Hankie, it's very confusing."

"It's not confusing at all. In fact, it's very simple. I'm a dog, you're a cat. I don't like cats, you don't like dogs. We thought we were going to die together, but that didn't work out, so now we'll have to live together...and, Pete, we'll go right back to the same lousy relationship we've enjoyed all these years."

"It has been nice."

"It's been a great lousy relationship. We've given it the best years of our lives. Let's don't mess it up."

He licked his paw with long strokes of his tongue. "I hear what you're saying, Hankie, but I must deliver some bad news." He stopped licking his paw and gave me a smile. "You did a good job and saved my life."

"I'm sorry. I apologize. It was an accident. I

to
mu
his
deed
"I

was under stress. I didn't know what I was...stop staring at me!" I leaped to my feet and began pacing. "No!"

"Hankie, I owe you a good deed, and there's not one thing you can do about it."

"That's where you're wrong, kitty. I won't allow it. As long as I'm Head of Ranch Security, we will not tolerate friendly relations between cats and dogs!"

He shrugged and grinned. "It's out of your hands, Hankie."

I marched back to him and melted him with a glare. "Okay, Pete, let's talk deal. I hate doing business with you, but this thing has gotten way out of control. What would it take to get us back to square one?"

He fluttered his eyelids. "Well, Hankie, I'm fond of scraps."

"Scraps? Great idea, no problem. Shoot me a number. How much are we talking about?"

"Oh, three scrap-days would be nice."

"You're covered."

"Four days would be even nicer."

"That's too many, but I'll take it."

"And, you know, a week would be ever so nice."

"Crook! I'll take it, and I hope you get indigestion."

"Thank you, Hankie." He twitched the last two inches of his scheming little tail. "But it won't change anything. You did a good deed and there's no going back. I have to return the favor, and until I do...we'll have to be on the same team."

My body was quivering with righteous anger. "Are you trying to ruin me?"

"It's a matter of honor, Hankie, not choice."

"You're determined to go through with this treachery?" He nodded. "Then do me one favor. Don't tell anyone, and for crying out loud, don't behave as though we're friends."

He was laughing again. "I'll see what I can do, Hankie, but I have to tell you something. The madder you get, the better I like you."

"I should have let the coyotes eat you."

"We're bonding, Hankie."

"You're sick. Do you hear me? Sick! I've got to get out of here before I'm as nutty as you are. Goodbye."

I rushed away from the little reptile, but his voice followed me. "When you need a favor, Hankie, I'll be there."

I whirled around and stomped back to him. "You know what breaks my heart about this fiasco? We had it made, Pete, we had everything going our way, and now you've let one good deed ruin it all. Goodbye...and don't ever speak to me again!"

I heard him laughing. "Hankie, you're a piece of work."

"And you can forget about the scrap rights!"

Do you find this confusing? I did. My brains were scrambled. What a mess! My assistant had been kidnapped by coyotes, the cat was threatening me with friendship, and I was exhausted from lack of sleep.

What more could go wrong?

Well, I could have run into a feather-brained rooster, and that's exactly what happened. Nobody expects to encounter a rooster in the middle of the night. Nobody wants to encounter J.T. Cluck in the middle of the night, but here he came, charging out of the chicken house, clucking and flapping his wings. "The British are coming, the British are coming!"

I ducked my head and made an abrupt turn to the south, hoping he might...I don't know, think I was someone else, I suppose. That flopped, of course, and he came at a run.

"Oh, there you are! It's about time you showed up. I need to turn in a 911."

"My shift was over three hours ago."

"Well, too bad." He caught his breath and glanced around. "Listen, pooch, Elsa woke up in the night and thought she heard strange noises."

"Yeah? So did I."

"Sometimes she hears good, but sometimes she gets confused. A guy never knows for sure. Remember the time she woke up and said she had a bull snake in her bed?"

"No. I missed that."

"Well, in the middle of the night, she flew out of bed and come over to me, clucking up a storm. Sometimes she gets hysterical, you know."

"Hurry up."

"About half the time, her clucking don't mean anything, but this time, she was mighty stirred up. She said, 'Oh, my goodness! Oh, my gracious! Oh, J.T, oh my!'"

"Look, pal, I'm busy. Could we talk about this another time?"

"I'm a-getting there, I'm a-getting there. So I said, 'Honey, settle down. What is it?' And that's when she told me about the snake. She said there was a great, big, huge, eight-foot bull snake in her nest."

"Get to the point."

"Huh?"

"Get...to...the...point!"

"Oh. All right, here we go." He stood on one leg and leaned closer. "Well sir, I had my doubts, figured she'd just woke up from a bad dream, but I went over and checked. And you wouldn't believe what I seen."

"You saw a great big huge eight-foot bull snake in her bed."

"No, he was only a six-footer...but how'd you know it was a snake?"

"You just told me."

"I did? Huh. Well, sometimes I repeat myself."

"I've noticed. Hurry up."

"Well, she had a snake in her bed, sure 'nuff, and that snake had swallowed three eggs whole. They can do that, you know, them bull snakes. Somehow they can unhinge their jaws."

"What happened?"

"Well, I gave that snake a whipping, is what I done. Heh. Yes sir, I worked that old general over with wings and pecks. Spurred him too, and he couldn't wait to get out of there. But we never got the eggs back."

I heaved a weary sigh. "J.T., if you came to tell me that Elsa heard coyotes, you wasted your time. I heard them too. They were real, I saw them, but they're gone. Go back to bed."

He stared at me. "Huh. Well, she's got pretty

good ears, for an old gal. I'll have to remember that the next time she sounds the alarm."

"Good night." I started walking away.

"Hold on, mister. What happens if them coyotes come back? You're the guard dog around here, and every chicken on this place has a right to know what you're going to do."

I walked back to him. "You want to know my plan?"

"That's right, pooch."

"All right, pay attention."

"I always pay attention. I'm the head rooster."

"Hush. I plan to hike down to the gas tanks and fall into my bed. If the coyotes come back, I will be sound asleep."

His eyes popped open. "Well, that don't sound good."

"If they raid the chicken house, I will still be asleep. In other words, J.T., you're on your own. Have a nice day."

"Now hold on just a second, mister. What am I supposed to tell Elsa? She's all stirred up and can't sleep."

"Tell her, 'Honey, shut your big yap and go back to bed.'"

He let out a gasp, and his eyes almost popped out of his head. "I ain't about to tell her that! You tell her."

"My shift is over, pal, and I'm gone. Good night."

I turned and walked away. Behind me, J.T. let out a squawk. "Some guard dog you turned out to be!" He continued to squawk and complain, but I couldn't have cared less. I was exhausted and haunted by the thought that my little pal had been kidnapped by cannibals.

CHAPTER SIX

I Try To Communicate With Slim

In spite of the best efforts of Pete and J.T. Cluck to disrupt my life, I made my way through the darkness and arrived at the Security Division's Vast Office Complex around 4:00 a.m. I rode the elevator up to the twelfth floor and went striding into my office.

OUR office, I should say, because for years, I had shared this space with Drover. Now, in the wee hours of the morning, I noticed the silence and emptiness of the place—his absence.

I scratched up my gunny sack bed and collapsed. My body cried out for sleep, but my mind refused to shut down. I lay there for what seemed hours, torturing myself with half-forgotten mummeries of the little geef who had swerved as my Assistant Snork of Rumple Stillskin.

I marimbaed the door...I remembered the day we first murked...first met. Barking wheezer figgie pudding funny little mutt who was a-skeetered of his own shallow...scared of his own shadow, let us say, and purple carrot feathers in the astonishing turnip tops...zzzzzzzzzzzzzzzz zzzzzzzzzzzzzzzzz.

Wait. I must have drifted off to sleep. Yes, I'm almost sure I did. Perhaps you notice that my narration...those paragraphs you just read...did you notice anything unusual about them? Viewed from a certain angle, they might appear to be... well, rambling and incoherent. In other words, the evidence suggests...

Okay, I was so worried about Drover that I couldn't sleep a wink, only I'm beginning to suspect that I did sleep a wink...several winks, in fact, and a lot winker than I ever thought possible.

That doesn't mean I wasn't frantic with worry about Drover. I was, but a dog is only a dog. Even the Head of Ranch Security is made of mere flesh and bones, and when our weary bones get deposited upon a gunny sack bed, by George, we fall asleep.

It's no disgrace, and history is filled with

examples of great heroes who fell asleep every once in a while. George Washington slept at Valley Fudge. Abraham Lincoln slept at Gurglesburg. Lassie and Old Yeller spent half their lives sleeping on the porch, and nobody ever called them slackers.

Sleep is a natural result of being awake too long, and the asleeper you get, the awaker you're not. I refuse to feel shame or to apologize for falling asleep.

Now, where were we before we got onto the subject of sleep? I have no idea.

It's a well-known fact that sleep knits up the rumpled sleeve of care, but sleep also rumples the knitting of your...whatever, and we were discussing something very, very important. It burns me up when I can't remember...wait! I've got it now.

Drover. My little pal had been kidnapped and hauled off to the wilderness by cannibals. I hardly slept a wink and didn't wake up until the crack of noon.

Now we're cooking. I came roaring out of a troubled sleep, leaped to my feet, and shouted, "Drover, wake up, we've got to rescue Drover from the coyotes!" I blinked my eyes against the glare of the sun and glanced around the office...and suddenly felt the huge emptiness of the place.

Drover was gone. I had to find him before the coyotes ate him for supper.

You think coyotes won't eat a dog? Ha. They eat poodles like candy. Ask anyone who lives on the edge of town. If your poodle leaves the yard and goes prancing off into the pasture, he's liable to end up as a coyote sandwich. Drover wasn't a poodle, but I had every reason to suppose that... well, we had Snort's own words as proof. Remember his parting words? "Coyote make yum-yum out of little white dog, oh boy!"

Recalling those awful words, I felt a wave of dread washing over me like a wave of dread. I had to do something...but what?

At that point, it occurred to me that my best hope of saving little Drover would be to get the cowboys involved in the case. Why? Because coyotes have a natural fear of people and will flee when one of them shows up.

Fleeing coyotes are much easier to deal with than coyotes that don't flee, don't you know. Coyotes that don't run are inclined to attack, beat up, and eat ranch dogs who show up to save their friends, so you can see that having a human along on a Search and Rescue can cut through a lot of red tape.

Slim Chance was just the guy who could provide cover for the operation. All I had to do was convey the message that Drover was missing and that I had a powerful need for his help.

Slim's help, that is, not Drover's. Drover seldom provided help for anything, and now that he was missing in action, he would be even more unhelperly. Even less helpful, shall we say, and maybe this is obvious, so...just skip it.

The point is that I left the office and went charging up the hill to the machine shed. There, I found Slim Chance, the hired hand on this outfit, changing the oil in his pickup.

To be more precise, he was sitting on an overturned five-gallon bucket, waiting for the oil to drain out of the motor. Whilst he waited, he cleaned his fingernails with his pocketknife and hummed a tune. "Doe dee doe dee dee doe." In other words, he wasn't doing much of anything, so this would be an ideal time for me to approach him.

To solicit his help in this deal, I chose a program we call "Something's Wrong," and here's how it works. You approach the person with Looks of Distress and switch the tail over to Slow Worried Wags. If he doesn't respond right away (on this ranch, they seldom do, I mean, we're talking about cowboys who are out to lunch half the time)...if he doesn't respond right away, we switch on Whimpers and Moans. WAM usually snags their attention.

I started the program and went into Stage One, Looks of Distress. Slim didn't notice (no surprise there), so I punched in the commands for Slow Worried Wags and activated the tail section. It was a great presentation and everything worked slick, yet Slim was so deeply involved in giving himself a manicure, he didn't notice.

Okay, I dialed in the codes and activated Stage Three, Whimpers and Moans. At that point, our entire program for recruiting volunteers was rolling, and let me pause here to point out something that you might not have noticed. In fact, you might want to take some notes on this.

See, when a highly-trained professional cowdog does a presentation of "Something's Wrong," a casual observer might get the impression that it's easy, that any old ranch mutt could pull it off. Ha. That's far from the truth. The truth is that "Something's Wrong" is an extremely difficult application that requires precise coordination of facial expression, tail movement, and special audio effects. The slightest error can produce wild distortions of the message.

I know, this seems complicated, so maybe I should provide a few examples. Pay attention.

Let's suppose that the dog gets the face right and the tail right, but hits a sour note on Whimpers and Moans. It can blow the whole program, and instead of transmitting the "Something's Wrong" message, you get some kind of garbage message, such as:

A. "Something's Right"
B. "Everything's Right"
C. "Nothing's Wrong"
D. "Everything is Nothing"
E. "Right is Wrong"
F. "What's For Supper?"
G. "Can We Play Ball?"

If that happens, the dog might as well pack up and go home, because his chances of recruiting help will drop to zilch. That's why it's so very, very important that we train for these exercises and get the coordination of all three stages just right.

Sorry, I didn't mean to go into so much technical detail about my work, but you'd be surprised how many people—and even dogs— aren't aware of just how difficult and complicated these "simple" presentations are. When we do it perfectly, it looks simple and easy, but now you know the truth: it's not.

Okay, I had activated all three stages of "Something's Wrong" and was waiting for Slim to respond. You know what? It went right past him, I mean, like a dove on the first day of hunting season. The guy didn't see any of it! I couldn't believe it.

When "Something's Wrong" flops, we have no choice but to go to Sterner Measures. I hated to do that, but the clock was running on this deal. We needed to locate little Drover and bring him back home—fast. I drew in a huge gulp of air and barked.

That woke him up. His mind had been far away, but it came rushing back to the present. He flinched and his head snapped into an upright position. He glared down at me.

"Meathead, don't bark when a man's cleaning his nails with an open blade."

Sorry.

"I could have chopped off a finger."

We need to talk.

"You've got no more manners than a goat."

Something's wrong. I need your help.

At last, he looked into my eyes. "What are you trying to say?"

Something's wrong and I need your help!

"Oh, I get it."

Well, glory be. It sure took him long enough.

He pushed himself up to a standing position, put away his knife, and...why was he walking into the machine shed? Drover was out in the pasture, not in the barn. Moments later, he emerged, carrying a red coffee can filled with Co-op dog food. He dumped it into the overturned Ford hubcap that served as our dog bowl.

"There. Eat it and dry up." He slouched back to his bucket-seat, flopped down, and resumed his silly exercise of cleaning his fingernails and listening to the drip-drip of motor oil.

Oh brother. How do you communicate with these people? If I had been trying to tell him that the ranch was on fire, he would have been barbecued alive.

Okay, he'd left me with no choice. I would have to do something really...huh? Before I could do anything outrageous to get his attention, an unidentified pickup pulled up in front of the machine shed.

All at once, I found myself pulled into a Traffic Alert. I rushed toward the vehicle and unlooshed a withering barrage of barking.

You'll never guess what happened then. I guarantee you won't.

CHAPTER SEVEN

A Cow Swallowed
a Bone

When we're called out on Traffic, we're never sure whether we'll encounter trespassers or Friendlies, and we have to assume the worst until we can get a positive ID. We treat them all the same. We rush to the scene with Sirens and Lights, and bark until Data Control gives us the order to stand down.

In this case, it came pretty quickly. The pickup matched our profiles of a Friendly and the driver turned out to be...well, the guy who owned the ranch, Loper. I switched off Sirens and Lights and rushed around to the left side of the vehicle to greet him the moment his boots touched the ground.

You probably think that my presence filled his

heart with joy, and that he greeted me with smiles, kind words, and pats on the head. Ha. Not only did he not smile or speak, I don't think he even saw me. He wore a deep scowl and his eyes were locked on Slim, who sat on the bucket with one leg thrown over the other knee, and was cleaning his fingernails.

Loper walked toward him. "I hope I'm not interrupting anything important."

"I'm waiting for the oil to drain out of the crankcase."

"How many days is that going to take?"

Slim sighed and looked up. "Loper, dirty motor oil don't ask my opinion of how fast it ought to drain. It moves slow."

"Well, we picked the right man for the job."

"Would it make you feel better if I stood up and led cheers to make it run faster?"

Loper said nothing, just stared. Slim stood up and...hang on, this is going to sound weird...he started doing a little dance, like a cheerleader at a football game.

"Lazy oil, run run run!
Lazy oil, fun fun fun.
Gush and rush like falling rain,
Faster, faster, down the drain!"

Loper shook his head and gazed off into the distance. "Am I paying you wages to do this stuff?"

"That's right, and it's a bargain too. I ain't charging you one penny extra for the cheerleading. It's all part of the package."

"Lord, have mercy."

"Loper, what's at the root of all this is that you don't trust gravity. See, oil obeys the Law of Gravity. It was all worked out years ago by a famous scientist, Sir Isaac Neutron."

"No wonder you flunked the ninth grade."

"And what he said was that oil drains out of a crankcase at a certain rate. It don't change from one day to the next, and it don't care what you think."

"Get in the pickup, we've got a job to do."

"What did you tear up this time?"

"We've got a cow with a bone in her throat."

Slim gave that some thought. "Well, we'd better get the horses up."

"Don't have time for that. I'm supposed to meet Bobby Barnett in town at three. I'm hoping we can lease his wheat pasture."

"Loper..."

"Hurry up, let's get this over with."

Loper headed for the pickup. Slim followed, muttering under his breath. When he opened the door on the passenger side, guess who was right there, coiled like a loaded spring and ready to leap into the cab. Me.

Hey, I knew they would need my help, and... well, Loper had said something about a bone, right? It just happened that I was the ranch's leading expert on bones. I leaped inside and claimed my usual spot beside the...

"Move, dog."

...shotgun-side window, only Slim hogged the spot and I had to move over to the middle of the seat. He climbed inside and spoke to the driver. "Did you want to take the dog?"

Loper's eyes flicked from me to Slim. "Sure, why not? Sometimes I get to craving intelligent company."

Slim cackled a laugh. "Loper, I'll swan, you beat anything I ever saw."

Off we went. We turned right at the mailbox, then took a feed trail that led to the north pastures. After a period of silence, Slim said, "How'd she get a bone in her throat?"

"I guess she needed some calcium and started chewing on a bone."

"Put out some mineral blocks."

"We'll put out mineral blocks, but she's still got a bone in her throat."

Slim nodded. "Well, what's your plan? The last time I checked, most cows won't stand still while you stick an arm down their guzzle to pull out a bone."

"We'll pitch a rope on her and tie her to the pickup."

"A grown cow? Loper, I've been to this rodeo before and what I remember is a wreck."

"She's weak. We can do it, trust me."

"We should have brought horses."

"We won't need horses."

On and on we drove over rough pasture roads, until finally we came to that old wooden windmill in the northwest pasture. Up ahead, I could see a cow standing alone beside the stock tank—actually between the stock tank and the overflow pond.

What is an overflow pond? I'm glad you asked. It's a small body of water, maybe fifty feet across, that catches the overflow water when the stock tank gets full.

It was easy to see that we had a problem here. When you find a cow standing off to herself, away from the other cattle, you can almost bet that something isn't right. Cows are herd animals. They stay with the bunch and don't like being alone.

That was my first clue in this case. The second clue came right on top of the first one: she looked thin and poor. For several days, she hadn't been able to eat or drink. Her flanks had a sunken appearance, which made her hip bones stick out, and her hair looked rough.

She was in sad shape, and if we didn't get that bone out of her throat, she would become coyote bait.

Wait, hold everything. Hadn't I been working a case that involved coyotes? I felt almost sure that I had, but somehow the details escaped me. I glanced over the notes and messages that were pinned to the bulletin board of my mind. I found several notes, but none that related to coyotes.

You want to take a peek at some of those messages? I can tell you that very few people or dogs have ever been invited to view the Security Division's bulletin board. A lot of those messages are highly classified, don't you know. In other words, this is a rare privilege. I probably shouldn't go public with this information, but maybe it won't hurt anything.

Okay, we'll start up here in the upper left hand corner and work our way down. You ready?

"Bark at mailman 10:00."

"Saturday: buried a bone in garden."

"Check for coons in feed barn."

"Cat made insulting remark."

"J.T. Cluck ate a roofing nail, got bad heartburn."

"Cat needs humbling."

"Talk to Little Alfred about sharing his cookies."

"Don't lick Sally May on the ankles. She hates it."

"Dreamed about Beulah. Wow."

"Dog bowl is empty."

"Saw bobcat tracks in corrals."

"Mailman came armed with squirt gun loaded with soapy water, shot me twice, what a rat. Tomorrow: double barking."

"Take bath, Emerald Pond."

"Don't jump on skunks. DO NOT jump on skunks!"

"Just finished patrol of chicken house, dying for a chicken dinner."

So there you are, a little glimpse at some of the messages that come through our office on a normal day. Oh, that last message, the one about the chicken? Ha ha. I don't know who wrote it, but it has no place on the Security Division's official bulletin board. Let's wad it up and throw it in the trash.

There, that's done.

Shameful. Outrageous. Whoever wrote that note will be punished.

Where were we? Oh yes, coyotes. As you can see, I had left myself no notes or messages about coyotes, so...I don't know where that leaves us. Maybe we should get back to the story.

Okay, this dunce of a cow had swallowed a bone and had gotten it hung in her throat, and if we didn't do something to remove it, she would wither away and drop dead.

That's probably what the old hag deserved. I mean, how dumb do you have to be to swallow a bone? But that's the kind of work we do around here, saving the lives of dingbat cows that are dumber than dirt.

Loper shut off the pickup motor and we watched the cow for a long time. Slim stroked his chin with one finger. Both men seemed lost in thought about the big project that faced us. As you will see, whatever thinking they did wasn't enough. Keep reading.

CHAPTER EIGHT

A Wreck

Slim broke the silence. "Okay, we've got .two cowboys, one rope, and one dog. How are we going to get the bone out?"

"You sit on the hood with the rope. I'll drive and give you a shot."

"Forget the hood. I'll ride in the back."

"You'd get a closer shot on the hood."

"Yeah, and if I fell off, you'd run over me, and probably enjoy it too."

Loper chuckled. "Fine, do it the hard way, I don't care. If you happen to slop a loop on her, dally the rope to the headache rack. We'll let her fight the rope till she chokes down, walk down the rope, open her mouth, pull out the bone, take off the rope, and go home. Ten minutes and we're done."

"We should have brought horses."

"Hurry up, will you? I've got things to do." Slim said no more. He found a catch-rope behind the seat, climbed into the bed of the pickup, and built a loop. When he had stepped outside the pickup and slammed the door, Loper muttered, "That is the slowest human being I ever saw."

Slim yelled, "All right, let's do it!"

Loper shifted into first gear and drove toward the cow. In theory, this promised to be an easy job: drive up close to the cow and pitch a loop around her neck. If cows were made of stone, cowboy plans would work every time, but cows are alive, and when a pickup comes toward them, they move.

She moved away as the pickup approached. Slim threw long and missed. He reloaded, made another long shot, and missed again. He was starting to get mad. "For crying out loud, get closer and give me a shot!"

"I told you to sit on the hood. Okay, hang on." Loper tromped on the gas and we roared after the cow. She ran, of course, but this time, Loper jerked the wheel to the left and stayed right on her tail. We waited for Slim to make his throw.

At that moment, we heard a racket coming

from the bed of the pickup. Loper looked through the back window. "Where'd he go?"

He seemed to be asking me. How was I supposed to know?

It was then that we saw Slim, picking himself off the ground. Gee, he must have fallen out. He slammed his hat down on his head and stomped over to Loper's open window. He didn't look too cheerful.

"Did you have to stick your foot plumb through the carburetor?"

"You said you wanted a close shot, I gave you a close shot. And I told you to hang on."

"Thunder, I didn't know you were going to play NASCAR."

Loper grunted and glanced at his watch. "I swear, it's hard to find good help these days."

"I agree, and since this was your big idea, why don't you show me how it's done?"

They glared at each other for a long moment, then Loper said, "By grabs, I'll take a piece of that. Five bucks says we'll be done and out of here in ten minutes—that is, if you don't mess up the driving too."

Slim shook his head. "Not five bucks, Loper. Ten."

"You're on, son. Kiss your ten goodbye." He

burst out of the cab. "Give me that rope."

He snatched the rope away from Slim. In a flash, he built a loop, made two quick twirls, and pitched a hoolihan loop around a clump of broom weed. He gave Slim a wink and a smirk. "That's how it's done in the Big Time. And I'll show you another trick. Pay attention."

He went to the front of the pickup and tied the home-end of his rope to the grill guard, then hopped up on the hood. "This is where you want to be when you rope out of a pickup. Can you drive without falling out of the cab?"

Slim barked a laugh. "Loper, you beat it all."

Slim started the pickup and we moved toward the cow. Up on the pickup hood, Loper had his loop cocked and ready to fire. Closer and closer. The cow watched us with an evil eye and shook her head. When she turned to run, Loper saw his shot.

In one rapid motion, he flicked out a loop that dropped over the cow's head and settled around her neck. He jerked the slack and turned around and showed Slim a grin that seemed to say, "That's how it's done."

Inside the cab, Slim muttered, "That was dumb luck. I think I just lost ten bucks."

It was a pretty piece of cowboy work, for sure,

but let me pause here to discuss some of the broader aspects of ranch management. See, if a top-of-the-line, blue-ribbon cowdog had been in charge this operation, he wouldn't have put troops into combat until he had answered one simple question:

"Is the pickup's grill guard stout enough to hold the jerk of a full-grown cow?"

It was a simple, obvious question, and the answer was absolutely crucial to the success of the mission, but I was pretty sure that neither Loper nor Slim had paused to ask it.

I knew these guys, I had worked beside them for years and knew how they approached a job of work. In a word, slap-dash. See, they'd exhausted all their mental assets figuring out how to pitch a noose around the neck of something big and mean, and had no mental reserves left to figure out what might happen if they succeeded—or, for that matter, how they might get their rope back.

Every cowboy should ask how he's going to get his rope back, but they seldom do. You know who wonders about such things? The dogs. See, for decades, loyal cowdogs have been sitting in ranch pickups, observing roping fiascos that turned absolutely bizarre. I mean, no circus master, no writer of comedy, no carnival owner could invent the scenes of chaos and mayhem that we dogs observe in the course of a normal day's work.

Just when we think we've seen it all, we find that we've seen only the beginning. There's more, always more.

Are you still with me? I hope so, because it's fixing to get wild and western.

Okay, when Loper tied the end of his rope to the grill guard, it never occurred to him to wonder if the bolts that held it to the frame of the pickup were worn and rusted. You'd suppose this might be a matter of interest, considering that 1) most ranch pickups are old; 2) ranch roads are rough and hard on bolts; 3) it sometimes rains and snows in the Texas Panhandle, and moisture is the leading cause of rust; and 4) bolts that are old, worn, and rusted tend to break under stress.

Loper didn't wonder about any of this. I, sitting in the pickup, wondered about it, but also knew that our people don't want to know what their dogs are thinking, so I sat in silence and didn't raise even a squeak of concern.

The most important question of the day was soon answered: No, the grill guard was not stout enough to take the jerk of a full-grown cow.

When she hit the end of the rope, we heard a loud, sickening CRUNCH. And two cowboys watched in amazement as the cow ran off, dragging the grill guard behind her. I was amazed that they were amazed. I mean, where do these guys live? What kind of cotton balls do they have inside their heads?

Oh brother.

Slim watched with an open mouth, then burst out laughing. "Good honk, will you look at that!"

Loper was nowhere close to laughing. "Don't just sit there. Grab the rope!"

Oh, the stories we dogs could tell if we only had a chance!

Loper bailed off the hood of the pickup and Slim exploded out the door, and the two of them sprinted after the cow. Well, this had turned into the disaster I had predicted, and I had let it go on long enough. I went sailing out the window. These yo-yoes needed help, before someone got maimed or killed.

Once on the ground, I kicked the jets up to Turbo Four, and began...I refuse to take the blame for tripping Slim. He was an adult male, a grown man, and should have been watching where he was going. My eyes were locked on the radar screen and, well, we had a little collision and he took a nasty fall.

Of course, he blamed ME. "Hank, for crying

out loud, get out of the way!"

See? I live with this all the time.

The chase continued. Loper was the first to reach the grill guard, which had now become a sled made out of steel pipe and angle iron. He jumped on it. A moment later, Slim arrived and jumped on it too.

Maybe they thought their weight would stop the cow, but they were wrong. She might have been thin and weak, but she gave the boys quite a ride, circled the windmill, and threw up a choking cloud of dust around the sled.

Flying blind through dust, I intercepted the beast just south of the windmill. I punched the targeting information into the computer and got a blinking red light to Launch the Weapon.

In this kind of combat situation, we target the nose, not the heels. Firing barks and bites at the rear of the brute will cause her to run faster, so when our objective is to stop the cow, we go for the nose. That's what I did, took a double-jawed bite on her nose and hung on.

That shut her down, and it gave Loper enough time to dig a knife out of his pocket. He managed to cut the rope and unhitch it from the grill guard. At last, we were getting a handle on this situation, but we weren't quite out of the woods yet.

The cow gave her head a mighty jerk and sent me flying through the air. Oof! I leaped to my feet and turned to face the...yipes, her eyes were flaming, and coils of steam hissed out of her nostrils.

She had decided to kill a certain dog. Me. And here she came!

Only a dunce would have stood there, waiting to see if she could do it. I whirled around and ran for my life, and within seconds, she was breathing fire on my tail section.

Perhaps you're wondering what the cowboys were doing while all this was going on. Great question, but you won't believe the answer. Loper grabbed the end of the rope, wrapped it around his hips, dug his heels into the dirt, and leaned back, with the apparent intention of stopping the cow.

I don't want to seem judgmental, but...what can you say? This was one of the DUMBEST stunts I had ever witnessed. What do you suppose happens to a one hundred and eighty pound rancher when a thousand-pound cow hits the end of a rope? I mean, it should have been obvious.

I suppose we can give him credit for being brave, but the result wasn't pretty. He got jerked out of his tracks like a tent peg, and was soon being dragged by the same cow that was trying to eat me. And she was getting closer by the second.

At that point, I did what any normal, intelligent, American cowdog would have done. I dived into the overflow pond, knowing that she would never follow me into the water.

CHAPTER NINE

Back On the Case

I'll be derned. She followed me into the water. She sure fooled me.

The good news is that I waded and swam across the muddy, stinking pond, and made it safely to the other side, turning a potential disaster into a triumph for the Security Division. The bad news is that Loper was still hanging onto the rope and got dragged into the pond.

Safe on dry land and dripping water, I barked a scorching message to the hateful witch. "And let that be a lesson to you! Cheaters never win and chinners never weep, and your mother was a cow!"

I got her told, didn't I? You bet. Even so, we weren't out of this deal yet. Don't forget our

original objective—not to go sled-riding or play in the water, but to remove a bone from the throat of a lunatic cow.

The pond wasn't deep, only two or three feet of nasty stinking water with a muddy bottom. Halfway across, the cow stopped. She couldn't breathe too well with that bone in her throat, don't you see, and she'd finally run out of gas.

She panted for air. Standing in water up to his thighs, Loper panted for air. Slim watched from dry land and tried to keep from laughing his head off. "What's your plan now?"

"Shut your gob!"

"I can handle that. Anything else?"

"Let's see if we can drive her to the windmill. We'll tie the rope to the tower." He waded toward the cow and waved his arms. "Hyah!" The cow stared at him with wooden eyes and gasped for air. She wasn't moving another step.

Standing on the bank and trying to bite back a smile, Slim said, "Well, maybe she'll stand still and you can snag the bone."

"Yeah? Or maybe you can get your skinny bachelor tail out here and help."

"Get in the water?"

"That's right, and you might want to hurry, before she gets her wind back."

Slim grumbled and muttered while he pulled off his boots and stripped down to his shorts. He waded out into the water and proceeded to "mug" the cow—threw an arm around her neck and held her tight, while Loper pried open her jaws and stuck his hand inside her mouth—pretty deep inside her mouth. The old rip had run out of fight and stood there through the whole operation.

Loper found the bone, gave it a jerk, and pulled it out. He held it up and gave it an inspection. She had gnawed all the sharp edges and it appeared to be in perfect condition for dog-chewing. My ears shot up, my tongue shot out, and my tail began to wag in wild anticipation. I could hardly wait for him to...

What a bummer. You know what he did with my bone? He pitched it over his shoulder, and with a splash, it was gone forever. It almost broke my heart. After all I'd done...what a waste of a good bone.

Oh well. Ranch dogs know a lot about broken hearts. We get one every two or three days. It just seems to go with the job.

When they waded to shore, they looked like two sea monsters slouching out of the Black Lagoon. Slim's shorts had turned brown from the muddy water, and he had green moss in his hair.

And Loper? Wow, what a mess—jeans, shirt, boots, hat.

They walked over to the stock tank and washed off the worst of the gunk with fresh water. As Slim slipped back into his jeans and boots, he said, "What time you got?"

Loper looked his wrist. "My watch is full of water."

"I'm guessing that you've missed your appointment in town." Loper said nothing. "And you owe me ten bucks. But I'll forgive your gambling debts if you'll do one little thing: admit that we should have brought horses."

Loper's face turned bright red, and he gave Slim a ferocious glare. "We should have brought horses. And when we get back to headquarters, you can start looking for another job." He stomped toward the pickup. His boots were so full of water, they squeaked and sloshed on every step.

Slim followed along in his cold-molasses walk, chuckling and shaking his head. "Loper, I swear, you're something else." I was walking beside him and he looked down at me. "Don't worry, pooch, he was only kidding about firing me. He knows it would take five men to replace me, and there ain't five men in the whole world who could stand his company for more than half a day."

Oh. That was good to hear. With those two jokers, you never know what to believe.

Well, we had survived the Bone Ordeal and, once again, I had pulled their chipmunks out of the woodchucks. I wasn't shocked or offended that they made me ride in the back of the pickup. After all, I was wet and muddy, and had acquired the stench of stale pond water.

Okay, it seemed a little unfair that they had singled me out. I mean, they smelled as bad as I did, but...oh well. Riding in the back was fine with me.

I took up my position of honor and seated myself in the middle of the spare tire. Loper put the pickup in gear and we started toward home. I was in the process of licking some of the water off my fur coat, when I happened to catch sight of something in the corner of my periphery. It wasn't much, just a flash of movement.

I turned my gaze toward the spot and took a closer...holy smokes, you'll never guess what I saw: two big scruffy coyotes! In fact, Rip and Snort.

Do you see the meaning of this? They'd been lurking in a wild plum thicket, waiting for their chance to make a meal out of old Bone In The

Throat. We'd messed up their supper plans, and now they were heading back to wherever cannibals go when they can't eat a helpless cow.

And suddenly I remembered what I'd been doing before I'd gotten drafted for this mission. I'd been preparing to go in search of poor little Drover, who'd been kidnapped by those same two thuggish coyotes! Maybe you'd forgotten about that, but not me. Okay, maybe I'd forgotten about it.

How could I have forgotten about it? Oh brother! Sometimes I wonder...never mind.

Well, the sight of the coyote brothers woke me up, and right away, I noticed a chilling detail: *Drover wasn't with them*, which meant: A) they had already eaten the little mutt, or B) he was sitting in a coyote dungeon, waiting for the evening festivities to begin.

I had to do something. Fast! My opportunity arrived when Loper stopped the pickup so that Slim could open a wire gate. I dived out of the back and set sail to the east, toward those deep canyons north of headquarters.

You probably think that my cowboy pals called and begged me to come back. Ha. They didn't even notice, and do you know why? Slim, Mister Songbird, had composed a funny little song about our ordeal with the cow, and he was singing it as they drove away.

Do you have any interest in hearing another of his corny songs? I guess it wouldn't hurt anything. Let's give it a listen.

Never Rope a Cow From the Hood of a Pickup

Now, me and Loper were driving around
The pasture and we found this cow
She'd swallowed a bone. Could we fix her up?
"Heck yeah," said Loper, and he's the boss,
"But we don't have time to saddle a horse.
Let's rope her from the hood of the pickup truck."

Without a brain to guide his steps,
He pitched a loop around her neck.
What followed then was just what you'd expect.
The grill guard flew off with the tug,
Me and Loper were getting drug.
Our lives were moving swiftly towards a wreck.

Never rope a cow from the hood of a pickup.
There's cheaper ways to get your thrills.
So cut that rope in thirty-seven pieces, boys.
You can't afford the doctor bills.

That cow was mad as an atom bomb.
She gave us a bath in a stinking pond
And a heck of a ride on a grill guard sled.
She done her best to kill us both,
You'd have to say, she came pretty close.
It would have made her day to see us dead.

Did Loper learn from woe and pain,
Not to pitch his loop on a moving train?
I doubt it and I'd say he flunked the course.
But there is a lesson here for them
That's smart enough to comprehend:
Park the frazzling truck and use a horse!

Never rope a cow from the hood of a pickup.
There's cheaper ways to get your thrills.
So cut that rope in thirty-seven pieces, boys.
You can't afford the doctor bills.

Well, it wasn't as bad as some of his songs. Actually, it was pretty funny, but the point is that they were so caught up in Slim's performance, they drove off and didn't even notice that they'd left me in the pasture.

Fine. I would have to finish the job all by myself.

I picked up the coyote scent right away. I didn't have the nose of a bird dog or the tracking instincts of a bloodhound, but let's be honest here: trailing a couple of flea-bag coyotes wasn't hard. They smelled so bad, even Drover could have tracked them. We're talking about a couple of guys who ate rotten meat, rolled on dead skunks, and never bathed.

So, yes, I picked up the scent right away and locked it into Snifforadar. The signal came in loud and clear. I set my speed at a long trot, a pace I knew I could maintain for several miles, and followed the yellow brick road of their bad smells.

On and on I went, over buffalo grass flats, up and down washed-out ravines, and across prairie country that was covered with things that were sharp and unfriendly—cactus, yucca, and cat-claw bushes. The farther east I went, the more the terrain began to change from rolling prairie country to deep unhospitalized canyons.

Deep INHOSPITABLE canyons. That's where you'll find the wild coyotes, in the deep inhospitable canyons, and the inhospitabler it is, the better they like it.

As I approached the mouth of Big Rocks Canyon, I stopped to rest. After catching my wind, I surveyed the country up ahead, and began to realize that...well, I'd been trailing these guys for half an hour but hadn't actually *seen* them. That seems odd, doesn't it? I mean, at some point in the Trailing Procedure, a guy ought to catch at least an occasional glimpse of ...unless they had...

Gulp.

Have you ever been all alone, but suddenly got a feeling that you *weren't* all alone? That was the feeling that swept over me as I sat there...all alone in a trackless wilderness, miles from house and home, and from anyone who might be able to come to my rescue.

I didn't want to look behind me. I'm not kidding, I did *not* want to look behind me, and a tiny voice in my head whispered, "If you don't look, you don't have to know."

That made sense, didn't it? Okay, it made sense for about five seconds, then it began to sound like something a dog might say to himself when he was scared out of his wits.

I had to look. I swallowed the lump in my throat, and slowly, very slowly, turned my head to see what kind of horrible creatures might be standing behind me.

You know what I saw? You won't believe this:

nothing! Nobody. In other words, I had creeped myself out with my own wild imagination. Ha ha. Boy, what a relief. That just goes to prove...I'm not sure what it proved, but it proved something very important.

Ha ha. Well, it was time to get on with the business of tracking cannibals and finding little Drover. I turned back to the east and walked smooth into Rip and Snort, and we're talking about bammo, in the blink of an eye.

There they stood, looming over me like a couple of pine trees. I was too shocked to be scared. My jaw dropped about three inches and I stared at them. They wore big toothy grins.

"Hey, where did you guys come from?"

"Ha! Guys come from following Hunk for long time."

"How could you have been following me? I was following you."

They howled with laughter. "Ha! Ranch dog dumber and dumbest for tracking to try coyote brothers."

"Yes, but...you can't do this." They laughed louder. "Do you know what this reminds me of? It reminds me of *cheating*. Yes, cheating—cutting corners and taking unfair advantage of a friend. You ought to be ashamed of yourselves. In fact,

I'm so upset by your behavior, I think I'll just leave."

I didn't think this would work, and it didn't. They darted into my path and blocked my escape. I would have to think of something else.

"Okay, I'll stay a while, but only if you'll agree to play by the rules. This cheating has got to stop."

That flopped. Snort pounded his chest and roared, "Rip and Snort gooder cheatest in whole world, not give a hoot for play by rules!"

"All right, let's go to the bottom line. I'm on an important mission to find my little friend, Drover." They stared at me. "Drover. Remember him? He's a dog, a small dog with a stub-tail, and you guys kidnapped him from ranch headquarters, remember?"

They held a whispering conference. "Kids not take nap, play all day, make noise too much."

Patience. I searched for patience. "Let's try another approach. This morning around four o'clock, you guys invaded ranch headquarters and tried to kidnap a cat."

"Guys tried to catnip kid."

"Right, that's what I meant, but instead of catnipping the kid, you kidnapped Drover."

"Little white mutt-mutt?"

"That's him. Is he…is he okay?"

The brothers exchanged grins. "Okay till sun goes down, ho ho."

Whew! Well, at least they hadn't eaten him yet. Maybe there was still hope.

CHAPTER TEN

I Put My Plan
Into Action

It appeared that Drover was still alive, but I had to figure out a plan for saving him. I continued my conversation with the cannibal brothers. "I'm here to deliver an urgent message from Drover's mother. She wants him to come home right away. He can't stay for supper."

Snort studied me with his empty yellow eyes. "What mother want with little white mutt-mutt?"

"Well, he's been gone all day. She...she's worried that he forgot to brush his teeth."

Snort shook his head. "Coyote not give a hoot for brushy teeth."

"All right, then consider this. It's way past his curfew."

Again, Snort shook his head. "Little mutt-

97

mutt got plenty kerchoo, sneeze all time."

"Exactly, and that's my whole point. He has bad allergies."

"Kerchoo all over coyote billage, spray spit-water on Rip and Snort."

"See? That's what I've been trying to tell you. He gets this way every year in the fall, sneezing his head off and blowing germs in all directions. And I'm sure you don't want his germs, so here's the perfect solution." I moved closer and lowered my voice. "Drover needs to take his pills. I'll rush him home and make sure he takes his allergy medicine, then bring him right back for supper. What do you think?"

I know this sounded crazy, but I was grasping at strawberries. When you're trying to do business with cannibals, you never know what kind of nonsense might work. Don't forget, those guys weren't normal.

They held another conference, then turned back to me. "Hunk talk too much."

"I know, but we want to get it right. I mean, you really don't want Drover sneezing on everyone during the big feast. Do we have a deal or not?"

"Hunk promise not telling big whopper to coyote brothers?"

Okay, at this crucial point in the drama, you're

probably thinking that I had worked myself into a corner, because everyone knows that the Head of Ranch Security can't tell a lie, right? I mean, when we take a Solemn Pledge, we have to stick to it, even if we're making the pledge to a couple of bloodthirsty coyotes.

Duty demands it. Ordinary mutts can tell whoppers, but Heads of Ranch Security are held to a higher standard.

It sounds hopeless, doesn't it? Heh. Not quite. Here's the clever trick I pulled on the coyote brotherhood—a trick, by the way, I had learned from Drover only hours before.

I raised my right paw in the air, stood at attention, and took a pledge. "Rip and Snort, ladies and gentlemen, honored guests: on this very solemn occasion, I promise NOT to NOT tell you a big whopperous lie."

Do you get it? Hee hee. I had promised to tell them a pack of lies, and they were so dumb, they fell for it, hook, line, and sewer. As I've said before, the mind of a dog is an awesome thing.

After whispering amongst themselves, they faced me again, and Snort said, "Brothers take deal, now lead Hunk to little white mutt-mutt."

I couldn't believe my luck. What a couple of dumbbells! They'd taken my deal and now they were going to deliver me right to Drover, which meant that I wouldn't have to waste any time looking for him. Hee hee!

Off we went into the deep dark canyon, Snort in the lead, me in the middle, and Rip bringing up the rear. I must say that it was rather pleasant. I mean, I'd been on a few adventures with these guys when...well, when tension filled the air. I had been under armed guard, in other words, and had been in fear for my life.

This time? Gee, it was like hanging out with a couple of old buddies. No threats or harsh words, no brute force or intimidation, just three happy guys, hiking through the canyons and enjoying the fellowship.

"Hey Snort, remember the time the three of us met at the silage pit? It was the middle of the night and you taught me how to eat silage. Then we sang your Coyote National Anthem. Remember?"

"Natchional Anthemum. Hunk talk right."

"Oh right, sorry. We sang your Natchional Anthemum. Remember?"

Snort grinned, warmed by the memories. "Uh! Snort remember pretty good. Hunk want to hear new coyote song?"

"Well, yes, sure, you bet. You got one in mind?"

"Got one in mind. Sing for Hunk and little friend at big supper feast, when sun go down and moon come up."

I smiled to myself. No doubt the sun would go down and the moon would come up, but Drover and I wouldn't be there for the "big supper feast." By the time Snort and the others figured out my clever trick, Drover and I would be far, far away. Hee hee.

Allergy medicine. Can you believe they fell for that?

But in the spirit of good will and friendship, I said, "That sounds great, Snort. I'll be looking forward to hearing the new song."

Hey, I was playing these guys like a couple of cheap fiddles.

We had now entered the canyon, with steep walls on both sides that rose three hundred feet, and a deep silence that you could only describe as spooky. This was home to the cannibals and a place where ranch dogs seldom ventured.

The coyote village—or "billage," as they called it in their native tongue—consisted of a collection of holes and caves, littered with bones, skulls, horns, toenails, scraps of hair, and other refuse left over from dinner parties of the past. I chose not to look too closely at the bones. I really didn't want to know how many of those bones might have once been part of a stray dog.

The village was also littered with scowling coyotes who paused from their normal behavior (scratching and fighting) to glare at us as we walked past. I put on a cheerful face and greeted them with a smile. "Hi, how are y'all? Nice afternoon, huh?"

Not a word of greeting, not a friendly smile, just brooding glares and cruel yellow eyes. Oh, and several of them licked their chops, which made me uneasy, and glad that I had a free ticket out of there. A guy wouldn't want to be in a place like this when the sun went down.

Near the center of the village, I looked around and saw a familiar face in the distance: old Chief Gut. He was coming toward us, limping on at least two of his skinny legs. He was easy to pick out of a crowd because of the notches bitten out of his ears and the old scars on his face. Several front teeth were missing, his ribs were showing, and he had a pair of eyes that you would describe as "bloodshot." They had red streaks.

That description might sound a little scary, but the truth was that old Gut looked like a joke on four legs. In his prime, he might have been a famous brawler and chicken thief, but now he was just trying to keep the old wreck afloat, as the cowboys would say. And, for a cannibal, he was a pleasant fellow. We'd met before, you know, and I'd always gotten the feeling that he kind of liked me. In another time and place, we might have become friends.

Here he came, limping and grinning. "Ah ha! Ranch dog come for bisit!" (That's the coyote word for "visit," don't you see). "Long time not see Hunk. Maybe stay for supper, huh?"

It's always a little unsettling when a cannibal invites you to supper. Even the nice ones might have hidden motives. I tried to hide my uneasiness and greeted him with a charming smile.

"Hi, Chief, great to see you again, and thanks for the invite. As a matter of fact, Rip and Snort have already invited me to the big feast and, yes, I'm going to attend...but first I have to run a little errand." He gave me a puzzled look. "Oh, maybe you haven't heard. I have to, uh, rush Drover back to the house and get his medicine. Allergies. He sneezes all the time. Kerchoo." I leaned toward him and whispered, "His mother insists. You know how they are."

The chief seemed perplexed by this, and he and Snort held a whispering conference off to the side. I heard them laughing and took that as a positive sign.

Chief Gut returned to me. "Okie dokie! Hunk take little white mutt-mutt to house and get kerchoo pills, hurry back for big supper feast in moonlight, oh boy."

"You bet. I'm really looking forward to it, Chief. We'll run as fast as we can and be back before dark."

He grinned and nodded. "Hunk be here for sure, ho ho."

Maybe I should have wondered what he meant by "ho ho," but at that very moment Snort jerked his head at me, which I interpreted to mean, "Hunk follow Snort and find little mutt-mutt."

It's kind of amazing that I was able to communicate so well with these goons, isn't it? You bet. But in my line of work, communication is extremely important. Why, if you don't know what the enemy is saying, you don't even know what he's saying, and that can get a guy in deep trouble.

I followed Snort to a cave in the west side of the canyon wall. This was the infamous coyote dungeon, the place where they held captives until...well, until supper was ready, I guess you might say. As we climbed over rocks to reach the cave, I studied the layout and committed every tiny detail to memory. You never know which one of those tiny details might come in handy later on.

I noticed one tiny detail that wasn't so tiny: there was no guard posted at the entrance, and that seemed pretty strange. What kind of dungeon had no guard? And what had prevented Drover from busting out of jail and making his escape?

It was then that the awful truth struck me. The poor little guy was probably bound and gagged, or maybe they'd chained him to the prison walls. Or maybe...gulp...this possibility hit me like a goose falling out of the sky. Maybe they'd already eaten him and this whole deal was a big hoax!

Were coyotes capable of this level of deceit? Because if they were, the Head of Ranch Security was walking straight into a death trap. The thought that I might have estumundered these brutes chilled me to the bone, but then...

I almost fainted with relief. Ha ha. You'll never guess what I heard. Drover's happy little voice, saying, "Okay, it's my turn."

Boy, what a relief! Sorry if I got you worked up over nothing, but when you go out on a dangerous mission with Hank the Cowdog, you have to expect a few chills and thrills, and a few bumps in the road.

I shouldn't have said anything about my deepest fears. I mean, it was crazy of me to think that I might have been out-smarted by a bunch of flea-bag coyotes. Those mugs could be dangerous if you got in their way, but at the level of heavy-duty thinking, they were no match for...well, for ME, you might say.

Everything was going according to my plan.

CHAPTER ELEVEN

Treachery On a Grand Scale

When I heard Drover's voice inside the cave, I felt a huge sense of relief. With Snort pointing the way, I rushed into the prison cell, expecting...well, I had every reason to suppose that the little mutt would be so glad to see me, he would spin in circles or something.

You know what he did? He looked up and said, "Oh, hi. What are you doing here?" And then he went back to playing Tug The Stick with a half-grown hoodlum coyote with sneaky little eyes and spiky teeth.

I was dumbfounded. I'd come to rescue the dunce, and he was playing games with the enemy? I stormed over to him and jerked the stick out of his mouth. "Give me that! On your feet."

"Gosh, what's wrong with you?"

"Hush and pay attention. Your mother is worried sick about you."

"My mom? Gee, I haven't seen her in years."

I used facial gestures, in hopes of alerting him to the fact that this was a top-secret communication. "We have to rush you back to the ranch so you can take your pills."

"What pills?"

"Your allergy medicine. You've been sneezing all over these coyotes and they're tired of it."

"Yeah, but we're having fun."

"Don't argue with me."

"And I don't have any pills."

My eyes were about to bulge out of my head. "Will you hush? Follow me, we're leaving."

He turned to the little thug he'd been playing with. "Sorry, Rowdy, I've got to go." I headed for the exit in a fast walk, but Snort was blocking the way. "Excuse me, Snort. If we're going to make it back for supper, we need to hurry."

I didn't like the way he grinned at me. I mean, we're talking about gleaming teeth and eyes that seemed to be dancing with cunning yellow light. He shook his head. "Uh uh. Hunk not go nowhere."

"What? Now wait just a second, Snort, we made a deal."

When Snort and the little hoodlum burst out in roars of mocking laughter, I began to suspect that I had been duped. Tricked. Sandbagged.

Snort looked down at me with cruel eyes and growled, "Ha! Hunk-dog dumber than dumb. Coyote not believe nothing about kerchoo pills. Hunk and little mutt-mutt friend stay for coyote supper, oh boy!"

I pulled myself up to a dignified pose and looked him straight in the eyes. "Snort, this is an outrage! I'm shocked beyond measure. Unless you release us this very moment, I will have to report this to the proper authorities."

This brought another explosion of rude laughter.

The kid, Rowdy, that smirking little hoodlum, left the cave. Staggering with laughter, he joined the mob outside and told them all about the incident. The mob roared and hooted.

Pretty depressing, huh? You bet, but it got worse. Snort stayed to guard the entrance. That was bad news. He turned his back on me and refused to talk, so I whirled around and roasted my pea-brained assistant with a flaming glare.

"Don't you see what's going on here? They're

going to eat you for supper!"

He gave me a dreamy grin. "Oh, they wouldn't do that, 'cause I'm their mascot."

"You're *what*?"

"They made me their official mascot."

I walked a few steps away to get control of my temper. I didn't want to scream in his face, not with Snort listening to the conversation. "Okay, Drover, let's try to calm down and take this one step at a time. Number one, you're *not* their official mascot."

"Well, they said I was. They had a contest and I won. They said I was the most popular doggie they'd ever met."

"Drover, you're sicker than I thought." I stormed over to him and stuck my nose in his face. "Listen, you little squeakbox, the guys who voted you Most Popular are *cannibals*. They lie and cheat and steal. They don't do it for a hobby. They're professionals, it's what they do for a living."

"Yeah, but..."

"If they ever had a mascot, do you know what they'd do with him?"

"Well, they said they'd take me on a nature hike."

"A nature hike! Oh brother. They're going to

eat you for supper, and the really sad part is, they plan to eat me too!"

His face went blank. "This is a joke, right?"

"If you're a coyote, it's a joke. If you're a dog, it's curtains."

"Gosh, you mean…you think they'd actually…"

"I don't *think*. I know. We're in deep trouble."

He collapsed on the floor and began kicking all four legs. "Oh, I feel so dumb! I believed all their lies and now they're going to eat me! I want to go home!"

"Yeah, me and you both." I sat there for what seemed hours, listening to him moan and sniffle. "That's enough. Stop blubbering. Pull yourself together."

"I can't stand it!"

"You have no choice. Stop crying. Look, if it will make you feel any better, I got suckered too." I told him all the details about my so-called rescue plan, which had become the Flop of the Century.

He stopped crying and stared at me with a goofy expression. "You thought they'd actually let me go back home to take an allergy pill?"

"Well…yes, and they seemed to have bought into it."

"I can't believe you believed they believed it.

That's the dumbest thing I ever heard."

"No, it's the second-dumbest thing you ever heard. The first-dumbest was that you thought a bunch of bloodthirsty cannibals had made you their Official Mascot. That is dumb-without-a-name."

He started sniffling again. "They seemed so sincere."

"They were sincerely lying. You got rolled, son." I heaved a sigh. "But so did I. The cruel fact is that neither one of us has anything to be proud of. Drover, this has turned out to be one of the darkest days our Security Division has ever experienced."

Speaking of dark days, I noticed that the world outside, beyond Snort's looming presence in the door, was showing the long shadows of evening. Down below, coyotes of all ages were yipping and howling, muttering, grunting, growling, grumbling, rumbling, and making all manner of grotesque noises.

They were getting themselves worked up for the evening's main event: us.

Gulp. We were running out of time. I had to do something, fast. "Hey, Snort, could we talk?" Silence. "Did you hear the one about the coyote and the parrot? Coyote walks into a cafe, see, and he's got a parrot on his shoulder. You'll love this. The waitress says, 'That's the ugliest bird I've ever seen. Where'd you find him?' And the parrot says...this will rip your stitches, Snort...the parrot says, 'He's not a bird. He's a coyote!' Ha ha! Did you get it? See, the bird was..."

"Hunk shut trap."

"Okay, let's skip the jokes and move to a more serious topic. Snort, we've talked about this before, but we need to talk about it again: the Brotherhood of All Animals. Search your heart and try to imagine..."

Snort whirled around, stomped over to me. "Hunk shut trap and listen to great new coyote song."

A new coyote song? Oh yeah, this must have been the one he mentioned earlier.

It was then that I began hearing the drumming and screeching outside. I had no choice but to listen. You want to hear it? It's pretty creepy.

A Creepy Coyote Song

Windmill turn in a restless wind.
Coyote pup in a canyon den.
Want his fresh meat medium rare.

Coyote call in the wind ain't there.

In the wind say the moon to the stars to the sky.
In the wind moan, bleach bone, don't know how.
In the wind, say the moon to the stars to the sky.
Coyote call in the wind not now.

Coyote stand in the pouring rain.
Coyote laugh till he look insane.
Not give a hoot, not give a care.
Coyote call in the wind ain't there.

In the wind say the moon to the stars to the sky.
In the wind moan, bleach bone, don't know how.
In the wind, say the moon to the stars to the sky.
Coyote call in the wind not now.

Coyote guy got a belly pain bad.
Here rabbit, there rabbit, hopping down the trail.
Gotta eat, gotta try, got a lot of loose hair,
Coyote call in the wind ain't there.

In the wind say the moon to the stars to the sky.
In the wind moan, bleach bone, don't know how.
In the wind, say the moon to the stars to the sky.
Coyote call in the wind not now.

Gotta eat!
Gotta try!
Gotta a lot of loose hair,
Coyote call in the wind ain't there!

What did I tell you? Was that a creepy song or what? Just imagine the effect it had on me and little Drover, locked inside a coyote dungeon. We didn't understand all the words, but we had a feeling that, somehow, the song was about...US.

Gag. I had goose bumps on top of goose bumps, and Drover...oh brother. He had moved past hysterics into a new realm of weird behavior. He was crawling around in circles, one moment giggling like a lunatic and the next minute moaning like a sick calf. Oh, and did I mention the sneezing? All at once he was sneezing, and yelping, "By allergies are killig be, help, burder, oh by lek!"

It was an incredible display of...who knows what? But it didn't do us any good. Snort stood like a dark mountain in the doorway. Our time was slipping away and we had lost all hope of ever getting out of this alive.

Should we go on with the story or just shut everything down? We've faced this decision before, you and I, and we've always managed to struggle through. But this...

Just think about it. Snort was blocking the exit. There was no back door to the cave (I'd already checked that out), and even if we'd managed to get past Snort, we would have run right into the mob of frenzied cannibals who were getting themselves tuned up for the evening's festivities.

It appeared that our geese were cooked.

CHAPTER TWELVE

The Ultimate Hoax

What's the deal? I thought we agreed to call it quits, but you're still reading. Maybe you were so worried about Slim and Drover that you couldn't sleep.

But wait! At that very moment, just when it was darkest before it got any darker, something very strange began to happen.

I heard a sound coming from outside the cave. It was faint at first, but it grew louder. I lifted my ears to MGM (Max Gathering Mode) and began pulling in the sound waves.

Snort heard it too. He cocked his head to the side and raised a pointed ear. Down below, outside the cave, the yelling stopped and an eerie silence crept like a shadow across the canyon.

In that deep, eerie silence, we heard a series of blood-chilling moans and cries, then a high-pitched voice that cried out:

**"I am the Ghost of Rabbits Past, Eaten by you like corned beef hash.
I see your grins and hear your drums.
I'll haunt you now till doomsday comes!!!"**

Wow. I thought I'd experienced goose bumps before, but fellers, this produced Goose Bumps Squared, and we're talking about cold chills piled on top of goose bumps on top of cold chills.

Every hair on the back of my neck stood straight up, from the end of my nose to the tip of my tail. Fingers of electricity skittered down my backbone, and for several moments, I forgot to breathe.

I had no idea what was going on out there in the canyon, but it was scaring the liver right out of me. What about Drover? Well, he fainted, and we're talking about spread across the dungeon floor like a gallon of spilled milk.

And Snort? He was shook up, fellers, trembling down to the soles of his feet, and his eyes had grown as wide as a couple of lemon meringue pies. He turned around to me, "Hunk make spooky sound?"

"No, it wasn't me. I don't know who or where it came from, but...Snort, have you eaten any rabbits lately?" He was too scared to speak, but nodded his head up and down. "How many?"

He raised his right foot, studied it for a moment, and held up three toes. "Umpty-seven."

"If I were you, I'd be sweating bullets. The Ghost of Rabbits Past is out there *looking for you.*"

He swallowed a lump in his throat. "Snort not believe in goats."

"Well, I guess everything is going to turn out fine."

At that very moment, the ghost let out a horrible screech of cackling laughter. Snort flinched. "Everything not turn out so fine." He pointed a paw toward the opening. "Hunk scram, feed goats. Snort stay here, hide in cave!"

"Me scram? Are you crazy? Look, pal, this is my dungeon. Go find your own. If you think I'm going to go out there with that ghost and let him..."

There had never been anything subtle about Snort. He snatched me up in his jaws like a rag doll and pitched me outside, and a moment later, he air-mailed Drover. We both hit the ground with a thud and rolled to the bottom of the hill.

I expected to be swarmed by all of Snort's kinfolks, but when I looked around, I saw nothing...nobody. They had vanished. Everyone was gone. Drover and I were the only living things left in the canyon...alone with a ghost that wanted to haunt someone until Doomsday.

I leaped to my feet and rushed over to Drover's side. "On your feet, son, we've got to make a run for it!"

"Can't do it, too scared, can't move, leg's killing me!"

"Fine, I'm leaving. You can stay here with the ghost."

He sat up and blinked his eyes. "You know, I'm feeling a little better now."

"Good. Hit Full Turbos and let's fly!"

Boy, you should have seen us! You talk about a couple of dogs burning a hole in the night air! I don't know how long it took us to make that two-mile run back to headquarters, but I can testify that we never slowed down and never looked back.

We arrived at ranch headquarters in record time, exhausted and gasping for air. We collapsed in front of the yard gate and were in the process of reviving our precious bodily fluids, when... guess who came slithering out of the shadows.

You probably think it was the ghost, and that he gobbled us down—teeth, hair, toenails, and bones, right there on the spot.

Nope. It was the cat. Pete. "Well, well, look who just arrived! And Drover has made his triumphant return to the ranch. How in the world did you get away from the coyotes?"

Drover started to answer, but I cut him off. "I'll handle this." I pushed myself up on all-fours and lumbered over to the gate, where the cat was sitting with his tail wrapped around his back side. "It was very simple, Kitty. One riot, one cowdog."

His face showed pure astonishment. "You mean...now Hankie, surely you didn't..."

"Beat up the coyotes? Ha. I thrashed 'em, Pete, wrecked twenty head of thieving cannibals. I gave 'em a few lessons in Dog Karate and they're all lying in a heap in the canyon."

"Really! Well, I'm just amazed."

"Biggest pile of coyotes we ever saw, right Drover?"

Drover frowned. "Well, that's not the way..."

"Hush." Back to the cat. "We left a huge pile of coyotes in the canyon, and I doubt that they'll ever want to mess with me again."

Kitty was still astonished. "Hankie, I hardly know what to say."

"Good. When the cats are speechless, the ranch is a happier place."

He stared at me and twitched the last two inches of his tail. "My, my. You didn't even need my help."

"Ha! You'd better believe it. Hank the Cowdog does not need help from the cats—ever. Now, go back to your spider web. Come on, Drover, our gunny sacks are waiting."

Pretty impressive, huh? You bet. Don't forget the old cowdog saying: "Do unto others, but don't take trash off the cats." In other words, do unto them before they can do unto you. Hee hee. I love messing with the mind of a cat.

And, well, that's pretty muchly the end of the story. Drover and I trotted down to the office, scratched up our gunny sack beds, and collapsed. Wow, you talk about a great bed! I stretched out my weary bones, closed my eyes, and...

"I am the Ghost of Rabbits Past!"

I flew out of bed. Drover flew out of bed. We found ourselves standing face to face in the dark. I whispered, "Did you say something?"

"No, it wasn't me."

"Okay, did you hear something?"

"Yeah, and I was hoping it was you, playing around."

"It wasn't me."

"Oh my gosh!"

"Eaten by you like corned beef hash!"

Drover's eyes bugged out. "It's the ghost! He followed us!"

My mind swirled. "Get control of yourself. We didn't eat any rabbits, so we ought to be okay."

"I see your grins and hear your drums."

"Hank, I've got a real bad feeling about this!"

"Right, me too. Okay, when I give the signal to move out, we will evacuate the building and take refuge in the machine shed." Zoom! Drover didn't wait for the signal. He was gone, out of there. "Hey, come back here!"

Drover had abandoned me, but the ghost hadn't. Yipes, he was still around. How did I know? I heard his horrible screeching voice—close!

"I'll haunt you now till dooms-day comes!!!"

Well, that was all I needed to hear. I tore up half an acre of grass and highballed it for the machine shed, went flying through the crack between the big sliding doors, and took refuge in the darkest corner.

Drover was already there, of course, shivering and clacking his teeth together. "Did the ghost follow you?"

"At this point, we don't know. We'll post a double guard. Nobody sleeps tonight, soldier. If he attacks, we'll go down fighting for the ranch."

"I'd rather not."

"Right, me either, but we'll just have to take what comes."

And so we began what promised to be one of the longest nights of our whole careers. Minutes passed, maybe hours, who could say? I had no trouble staying awake. I was wired with brute fear. Then...I heard a voice. It seemed to be coming from the front of the shed.

"Hankie? Drover? Yoo-hoo, anybody home?"

Whew! Unless I was badly mistaken, I had just heard the voice of the cat. Did I dare speak and expose our position? Yes. I needed to find out if he had crucial information about the ghost.

"Pete? Is that you?"

"Um hm."

"I must ask you a very important question."

"Oh goodie. I just love answering your questions."

"Pete, do you know anything about a ghost?"

"The Ghost of Rabbits Past?"

"Right, that's the one. Talk to me, pal, where is he?"

"Well, Hankie, he's right here."

My whole body went rigid. "He's in the machine shed?"

"Um hm. For you see, Hankie..." There was a long throbbing pause. *"I am the Ghost of Rabbits Past. Hee hee!"*

Huh?

"I did you a favor, Hankie, and now we're back to zero. Nightie night."

HUH?

Okay, we need to talk. That last page you just

read...we must do something about it. See, it contained Highly Classified Information—not ordinary Highly Classified Information, but Top Secret Keep-Your-Trap-Shut Highly Classified Information. The little children must never be exposed to these secrets, so let's do whatever we must to, uh, control the spread of the so-forth.

Can I count on you to plug all the leaks? Good, thanks. Sorry to bother you, but this deal came up all of a sudden and...

Never mind. The impointant point is that Drover and I survived the night and escaped a terrible fate by the tiniest of margins. We can attribute our success to vigilance, training, and iron discipline. If there's more to this story, you don't need to know about it.

This case is closed. And I mean CLOSED. Don't you dare mention this to anyone!

HANK
THE COWDOG®

Have you read all
of Hank's adventures?

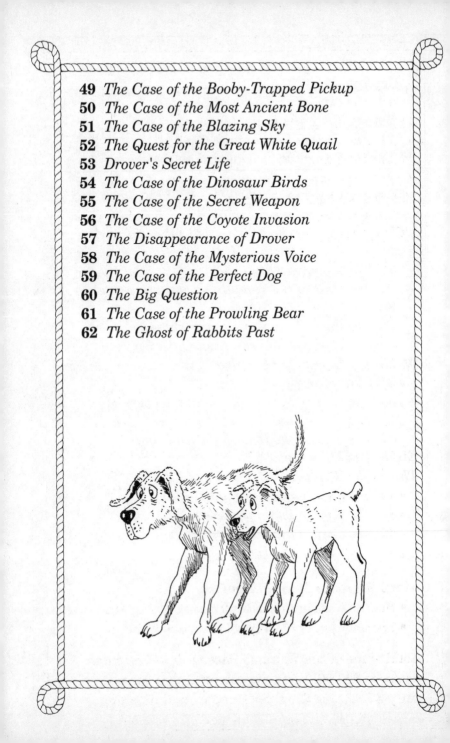

Join Hank the Cowdog's Security Force

Are you a big Hank the Cowdog fan? Then you'll want to join Hank's Security Force! Here is some of the neat stuff you will receive:

Welcome Package
- A Hank paperback
- An Original (19"x25") Hank Poster
- A Hank bookmark

Eight digital issues of
***The Hank Times* with**
- Lots of great games and puzzles
- Stories about Hank and his friends
- Special previews of future books
- Fun contests

More Security Force Benefits
- Special discounts on Hank books, audios, and more
- Special Members-Only section on website

Total value of the Welcome Package and *The Hank Times* is $23.99. However, your two-year membership is **only $7.99** plus $5.00 for shipping and handling.

☐ Yes I want to join Hank's Security Force. Enclosed is $12.99 ($7.99 + $5.00 for shipping and handling) for my **two-year membership**. [Make check payable to Maverick Books.]

Which book would you like to receive in your Welcome Package? (#   ) any book except #50

_____

BOY or GIRL

YOUR NAME   (CIRCLE ONE)

_____

MAILING ADDRESS

_____

CITY   STATE   ZIP

_____

TELEPHONE   BIRTH DATE

_____

E-MAIL   (required for digital Hank Times)

Send check or money order for $12.99 to:

Hank's Security Force
Maverick Books
PO Box 549
Perryton, Texas 79070

DO NOT SEND CASH. NO CREDIT CARDS ACCEPTED.
Allow 2–3 weeks for delivery.
Offer is subject to change.

And, be sure to check out Hank's official website at
www.hankthecowdog.com
for exciting games, activities and up-to-date
news about the latest Hank books!

Photo Courtesy of Western Horseman Magazine

John R. Erickson, a former cowboy, has written numerous books for both children and adults and is best known for his acclaimed *Hank the Cowdog* series. He lives and works on his ranch in Perryton, Texas, with his family.

Gerald L. Holmes has illustrated numerous cartoons and textbooks in addition to the *Hank the Cowdog* series. He lives in Perryton, Texas.

Shawn Tevis Photography